Fear and Fury

Adventures of a Villain-Leaning Humanoid

Book One

Jamie Jackson

CONTENT/TRIGGER WARNINGS

Psychic/Mental Coercion, blood & gore, sex and sexual acts, mention of drug use, kidnapping/forced restraint, torture, harsh language, mention of sexual assault/rape (none occurs)

CONTENTS

ACKNOWLEDGMENTS

Thank you to my husband, children, house and dogs for enduring serious neglect while I feverishly wrote the first draft.

Thank you to Jennifer, Jennifer and Jinna for suffering through reading that first draft.

And thank you to the cast and crew of The Mandalorian for inspiring me to write again.

CHAPTER ONE

I am the monster that lives inside your head.

Hold on, that was melodramatic. Let me start over.

I'm not the kind of person who should have been given superpowers. I'm hardly what you would call a hero. I'm not even sure I would qualify as an anti-hero. More like Peter Parker before he was Spiderman, when he committed that one selfish, petty act that led to his Uncle Ben dying. You know the scene in the first Spider-Man movie with Tobey McGuire? Where he lets the guy steal the cash from the dick who won't give him his prize money for winning that cage match? That one. No, I haven't read the comics. You're dragging us off topic. Unlike Peter, I didn't learn my lesson from it, and that's my attitude all the time. But I guess when your power is literally fear it's a little hard not to lean toward villainy.

Wait, we're getting off on the wrong foot. Hi, I'm Megaera, Meg for short. Look, don't ask me, my parents were HUGE on Greek history and mythology. I don't know why they picked it. I mean, it could be because the people the tales were about were real. Not gods, Jesus, they think they were the first heroes and villains. All the heroes of legend had powers. Beowulf? Real person. Grendel and his mother? Real people. Hercules? Real person. Gilgamesh? Real person. Want me to go on? Because I can. For a while the heroes and villains disappeared from the world, and then sometime in the 1940s or so, they started coming back. We're born with these abilities. Spiderman? No, he's not real, but for some reason no one wants movies and TV shows about us, just the made-up heroes.

What do you mean is New York real? No, it's made up too. I mean, they based it on Malus City, where I live, but no, it's not real. Are you okay? How many fingers am I holding up? Then stop asking stupid questions.

Hold on, we're getting off topic again. Where was I going with this? Oh, right. For the record, I don't go clubbing, I don't drink, and I don't do drugs. I mean, I tried them once at a party, and the results were, well, not good. For everyone else. You only need one unintentional bloodbath in your life, I think.

You won't find anything in the news about it. That got covered up. (You only get one!) Since then, it's been non-stop recruitment attempts from both sides. I remember there was this one – come on, say it dramatically with me – *evil-doer* who would just not leave me alone. Like, calling at all times, boombox outside my window, maggoty roses. Seriously, what is with that? Is that an "all villains" thing? He wanted us to rule the world together. Again, why? Do they not realize how much work that involves? It was like being stalked by Shaggy from *Scooby-Doo*'s evil twin. The boombox? Please tell me you've seen *Say Anything*. Oh, come on! It's a classic! It's John Cusack! You know what, never mind. Your own fault you're missing out. Stop changing the subject.

Villain boy did not like my response. But then again, I

didn't like his "don't take no for an answer" attitude, so, I feel like terrorizing him into ripping his own skin to shreds wasn't entirely undeserved.

I don't pull that shit with the heroes though. Villains don't really care about you killing other villains. Less competition, blah, blah, blah. Heroes, though, you kill one it's like stepping on a fire ant hill. The rest of them will come boiling out to bite and sting you, and they are relentless. It's bad enough that they're like Jehovah's Witnesses, constantly knocking on my door. "Have you thought about SAVING the world?" I mean, don't get me wrong, they're SUPER (haha, get it?) polite about it. But once they know where you live, and that you do answer the door (even if it's only occasionally and sometimes totally nude), they send someone by at least once a week to ask you that question.

Literally all I want to do is to be left alone, to live out my life, sometimes scaring the bejeezus out of the local Karens. Come on, you can't tell me that's not funny.

Yes, I work in customer service. Why do you ask?

Yes, it's retail. Again, is that part important? No, I'm not going to tell you where. I don't need you rolling up to my place of work. You want me showing up at your job and harassing you? Didn't think so.

Oh my God, fine, suffice to say it's a big box store. It's not Target, it's not Wal-Mart, and it involves some ugly-ass khaki pants and an oversized green polo for a uniform, and that's all I'm going to tell you.

I'm sorry, but you don't get to judge me for working a "dead end" job instead of risking life and limb to save the ingrates. I'm not bulletproof, unlike SOME people. Oh, one more thing, I've got a really big bubble, so I'm gonna need you to back on up out of my personal space. Little bit more. No, more. No seriously, more.

Anyway, on the dull, gray Tuesday morning our story starts (come on, you know exactly where that line is from!), I was working the customer service counter, and this guy walks in. You know how some people are just up to no good? They've got this, twitch to them? He was like that. There was nothing else physically about him that would've made me say, "Ooh, damn, things about to go wrong up in here." Just that you could tell he was nervous about something. And he wasn't a *villain* villain. Those you can spot from, like, a mile away. I think it's the spandex costumes.

I'm kidding. They don't really dress like that. Otherwise, it would make getting away with things a lot harder.

Back to the twitchy dude. I was trying to place him, because he looked familiar you know? Like, I should know this guy. I have to have met him before. And then he takes out a gun and starts waving it around while screaming at one of our cashiers, Lauren.

So now, of course, we have screaming customers and, security is nowhere to be seen. Like, what do we even pay you for, Chad?

So, I walk over -- yeah, I know, I just said I'm not bulletproof, and I don't do the hero stuff because I don't wanna die. Hold your horses. This was literally because once someone like that actually starts shooting, I'm at as much risk as anyone else of dying.

"Hey, Lauren. You and your boyfriend need to take this outside," I tell her.

They both stare at me.

"Meg, what the actual fuck? Why aren't you calling the police?!"

"That's Chad's job."

4

"I will shoot this cheating bitch; I swear to God I will!" the guy screams at me, and I place him. It's actually Lauren's boyfriend. Ha!

"Look, Mike, I don't care if you shoot her. Just take it outside. You're scaring the other customers and making MY job harder."

Lauren just stares at me, mouth agape. "Are you fucking serious right now?"

"Like a heart attack," I say cheerfully. "Seriously, take it outside." Even Mike is staring at me, like he can't believe I'm advocating him shooting her.

"What the fuck, Meg?" he says.

"Okay, so I'm getting tired of repeating myself. Take it outside, or else."

"Or else what?" His voice was shaking because it starts with the whispers. At first, it's just sighing, almost like the wind, then the giggles. If I let them go long enough, it escalates to the shrieking, screaming and howling.

"Or else my friends are going to get involved, and you don't want that," I say. The long black shadows on the floor are elongating, stretching, reaching, and the figures are brushing my shoulders, curling down my arms to flow through the air, their long-fingered hands grazing the floor.

Okay, so this is where it tends to get dicey, especially with people who are armed. It's exactly why I worry about getting shot, but Mike was pissing me off because the fucker just would not listen to me. Lauren, too, but if I did this to her, she'd piss all over the floor, and I am not cleaning that up. If the two of them had just stepped outside, I could've just hammered the fear into him right at the door with less risk of getting shot in the first place. Fortunately for me, at that point Mike ran instead of shooting at anyone. Regular people can't see the figures, but they can definitely sense them, and sometimes that results in firing in random directions. So, yeah, risky. I let the whispers, figures and shadows go. They faded away back into the ether they come from.

You know, it's the figures that convince me Hell is probably real. But since they seem to like me I'm not super concerned about it.

∞

Lauren got to leave early.

Okay, yeah, it was to go down to the police precinct to fill out a report or press charges? I don't know, I avoid going to the police altogether, so I'm not sure how all that works.

Still, she got to leave her shift early, and I got yelled at by the manager for not calling the police, for getting involved in the first place, oh, and also for being mean to Lauren. He also told me I'm lucky he wasn't going to fire me.

I mean, Jesus, people, I got him to leave and not actually shoot her, right?

See, this shit right here is why I won't be a hero. No gratitude for a job well done. And I did it without anyone dying. Let's see BulletProof pull that off. What with projectiles ricocheting off him to hit innocent bystanders for fuck's sake. (Okay, maybe that was only the one time. Not the point.)

Yes, that is actually his superhero name. What gave you the idea that they would be, you know, original? Also, you notice how none of *them* showed up to save Lauren? Yeah, typical. Because *they* have "bigger" problems to deal with. The only time one of you little people is gonna get saved by one of *them* is if they happen to run across you while you're in trouble. And if that happens, it's probably Vigilante, who I've heard of but fortunately haven't had the displeasure of meeting, because he LIVES for that shit. Everyone knows he works alone, so he hasn't tried to recruit me.

Other than that, y'all are on your own.

Ahem, moving on.

So, once my shift was actually over (Don't ask me why the store didn't just close. Gotta get that money, I guess!) and I got to leave, I got the unpleasant surprise of being approached in the parking lot. By a hero. In civies. Again, where was *he* while people were actually in danger? And yes, I can tell a hero from a non-hero. It's in the strut. I was barely out the doors when he came up to me.

This was a new development because usually they just show up at my apartment.

"Not interested," I told him. I only paused to check for cars; otherwise, I would've marched right by him. My brain registered tall, blonde, broad-shouldered, muscular, t-shirt, jeans, chucks, in that automatic-person-nearby-assessment way.

He looked startled. "I haven't even said anything yet."

"Yup, I know. I also know what you were going to say, and, like I said, not interested." I started across the parking lot because I needed to reach the bus stop up at the street. After the day I had, I didn't need to miss my bus on top of everything else.

"What was I going to say?" he asked, falling into step next to me.

"The world is in danger, blah, blah, blah. It's, like, weekly with you guys. At least the villains leave me alone now."

"Well, the world *is* in danger, and you have a unique set of skills."

"You know, I feel like that's not entirely true. So, like, go away."

7

"Which part?"

I stopped walking to face him, my chin raised, partially because I'm stubborn, and partially because I had to tilt my head back to look him in the eye. I've been told I look dainty, which I think is nice code for small, breakable and non-threatening in appearance. "Seriously? Do you not know how to take a hint? I'm not interested in joining any 'merry save the world' bands."

"Noted, but that isn't what I was going to say."

"Uh huh," I said skeptically. "You weren't going to do what every other hero who's been sent to talk to me did?"

"Nope."

"Then what the fuck do you want?"

"I wanted to ask you out."

I laughed. "I'm sorry, what?"

"I wanted to ask you to go to dinner with me."

"What, is this like a new thing now? Ask me on a date so you can trap me in public while you do your sales pitch?" I asked suspiciously.

"Absolutely not."

"Then what is it?" I wanted to know what his angle was.

"Literally just asking you out."

"Okay," I said. "The answer is no, so bye now." And I walked away. I don't date, heroes or otherwise. I don't need the complication.

He followed me. "Tell me why not."

I stopped again, turning to face him. "Pretty sure I don't owe you an explanation. No is no is no, which for supposedly being the good guys, you all don't seem to get."

"Huh," he said. "You might have a point."

"Tell me about it," I said, rolling my eyes. "So, once again, bye." I started back up the pavement.

"Wait," he said, rushing after me. "Could you just tell me over coffee why you don't want to join us? I swear, not to try and convert you. And not as a date. Just explain it, and I promise to get the other heroes to stop harassing you about it."

I stopped, considering. The offer was tempting. I'm not kidding when I say they're coming by weekly. Okay, sometimes it's not heroes. It's whatever poor greenhorn the military has fobbed the job off on that day. What? Who do you think pays their salary? You think they're just running around saving the world for free? No, there's an entire branch—wait, department? You know what, let's just go with branch—that oversees their operations. Of course that doesn't mean the heroes don't play loosey goosey with the rules. Are you going to be the one to tell the guy with the laser eyes that, according to his contract, he can't do that? Didn't think so.

Which made this an easy decision. "You swear it's not a date? Just coffee?"

"Just coffee."

"And you'll get the rest to leave me alone?"

"Absolutely. Can't make any guarantees that the villain harassment won't pick back up, though."

"Ha," I said. "After what I did to Mirage I doubt it." Yes, that's the evil-doer I mentioned earlier. Congratulations, you solved it. You want a cookie?

"That was you?"

"Who the fuck else can get people to tear their own skin off?"

"Well, Flayer—"

"Correction, Flayer peels your skin off himself. His victims do not do it to themselves." I know because he told me so himself when he invited me to join him. Said something creepy about how he wanted to watch them do it to themselves instead. I think he got the point when I made it clear I'm not into that.

The hero cleared his throat. "On that cheerful note, what's the next morning you have off?"

"Friday."

"Great," he said, "I'm free that day too. Well, I have any morning I want off."

"Uh huh," I said. Must be nice getting to demand whatever schedule you feel like following.

"Anyway," he said as he took a few steps back from me, "I'll pick you up at your apartment."

"You know where it is?"

"Yup."

"Of course you do."

"See you Friday." He smiled at me and took off. I mean literally took off because he flew straight up into the air. I had to cover my ears because of the sonic boom his wake created.

"Great," I grumbled. "That better not be how he picks me up."

∞

There was an insistent knocking sound. A rapping noise loud enough to wake me up. Blearily I opened my eyes, my head was facing my bedroom door. My apartment is done in those typical beige and brown colors because the landlord is cheap. So, looking at my door didn't tell me anything of interest. And it was too early to be up.

"Go away," I muttered, pulling the pillow over my head and hoping whoever was knocking would get the message.

The noise didn't stop.

"Go away." I tried a louder volume. That didn't work

either, so I sat up and yelled, "GO AWAY!"

I was greeted by the sight of the hero from the parking lot at my window. Considering I live in a third-floor apartment, this was not a normal occurrence, even with heroes constantly bugging me. I jumped out of the bed and scurried over to the window. "What are you doing?!" I hissed at him as I opened it. "It's bad enough my neighbors think I'm in some sort of program or a dealer. What the fuck are they gonna think when they see people floating outside my window?!"

"Hello to you, too," he said, climbing in through the window. "I tried your door first, but you didn't answer, and after fifteen minutes I was starting to get looks from the people next door to you."

"So, you thought my window was going to look better than that?"

"Well, I didn't want them to think I was a bad kind of guy."

"Uh huh. And you still think the window would look better?"

"Better than me breaking down the door to make sure you weren't dead. I wouldn't want you to lose your security deposit."

"Har-dee-har-har," I said. "Why are you here?"

"We're supposed to get coffee together, remember?"

"Damn it," I said. I had been hoping he would forget, end of hero harassment, promise or not. "Okay, look, go wait in the living room or something so I can shower." He headed out my bedroom door. "And don't go looking through my stuff!" I yelled after him.

I took the time to wash my hair. It's long, thick and curly, I mean, we're talking tight, bouncy ringlets that I can't just brush because otherwise I look like a damn poodle, and it takes forever to wash and dry. But I was going to make him wait on me because I was hoping he would get tired of twiddling his thumbs and leave. Then, just to be a brat I got it tamed back into a ponytail.

And now the real question, makeup or no makeup? Makeup would mean he waits longer, but I don't want him to think I'm putting in any effort for him. Foundation is a pain in the ass anyway, I can never pick the right shade. I've got Mediterranean coloring, so I constantly look tanned. My parents may or may not have been so into Greece because of their ancestry. Like *My Big Fat Greek Wedding* levels of love. What were we talking about? Oh yeah, makeup. Eyeliner is even worse. I have grey eyes, but the shade constantly shifts from light to dark. They look almost black when I call to the whispers. I know because I've done it and then looked in a mirror. You can't tell me you wouldn't be curious, too.

So yes, I vacillated for a while on the subject of makeup and decided on going bare-faced. What? It takes time and effort to be this inconsiderate.

When I finally came out, I was dressed in ripped skinny jeans, a tank top and knock off chucks. What? Did you think I was going to dress up for him? If I had sweats, I would've dressed down even further. He was still in my apartment, sitting on my couch, head cocked to the side. Damn it.

"What are you doing?"

"Your downstairs neighbors are arguing about whether gnocchi is made of potatoes."

"So, you eavesdrop too?"

"I can't really shut it off, and sometimes you hear some useful stuff."

"Uh huh. Are we going? Actually, where are we going?" Look, I don't get out much. I go to work, I go home, that's about it. I like to remain blissfully unaware of life outside my four walls.

"There's a coffee shop just down the street."

"So, we're walking?"

"I could—"

"Nope, nope, nope. Walking is fine."

We headed out the door and down the stairs before he said anything else.

"Are you afraid of flying?"

"No, I just don't want to be caught dead out in public with you." I'm not afraid of flying per se, but I don't owe him the whole truth. What? I don't know this dude from Adam. He's lucky I'm going anywhere with him at all.

He looked around us, at the people coming up and down the sidewalks. "We are going out in public."

"Yeah, but not like that, genius, because you're in civies. If you were in costume I would, one, refuse to go anywhere with you, and two, definitely wouldn't have let you in my apartment. So, if I let you fly me anywhere, EVERYBODY would know exactly what you are." Yes, the heroes wear costumes, unlike the villains, because they want people to be able to identify them. Not spandex though. At least, not that I've seen.

"You say that like you're not one of us."

"Because I'm not."

"Except you are," he insisted. "You've got powers, that makes you—"

"What? Unique? *Special?*" I said, with exaggerated finger quotes. "They don't make me better than anybody else; they just make me more dangerous. And by golly gee willikers does the world need higher numbers of more dangerous people in it!"

"So, you could help—"

"Nope."

"But—"

"Uh uh. You said, no trying to convince me."

We had reached the coffee shop, the sign above it declared the name *The Toasted Bean*, but didn't head in yet. Instead, we stood on the sidewalk, blocking the doors. He stared at me, hands in his pockets.

"Yeah, you're right. But you also said you would tell me why you don't want to be a hero. So why not?"

"Because I don't want to." I headed into the coffee shop and straight for the counter at the back. It smelled of, predictably, coffee. There were deep leather couches, wingback chairs, and little two-seater tables scattered around. All of it done in a mix of dark and bright colors, I think they went for eclectic but just ended up not matching. "Hey, medium roast, black, please."

"Sure, what size?" chirped the barista. Blond hair pulled back in a ponytail, huge smile on her face, black uniform with a black apron, and no name tag. She looked entirely too cheerful.

"I don't know, large? Do you have buckets?"

She laughed, and I found that annoying. I knew that I wasn't really annoyed with her, although her peppy attitude this early in the morning was grating. I'm not a morning person, so everything this early in the day is grating. Either way, she gave me a large cup of coffee.

"That'll be $3.47 with tax."

"Hold on," said the hero behind me, "I've got it. Can you add a whole milk cinnamon dolce latte to that order? Medium?"

"Oh my God," I said, casting him a side eye. "Are you serious?"

"I like lattes," he said.

"Snob," I said, stalking off to a table. I watched the barista flirt with him as she was getting him his drink. I snorted. I guess he's kind of cute if you're into that Archer-as-a-blond-pretty-boy look. And he did have a nice smile. What? I said I don't date, not that I don't look. I'm still human. Sometimes a girl has needs.

Once he had his drink, he came to sit down with me. I twisted his cup around, so the number and name written on it faced him. "Tiffany wants you to call her," I sneered. She had even put a little heart over the "i".

"I'm not interested in Tiffany." The expression on his face was serious. Okay, fine, I was being bratty; he's a tiny bit more rugged than pretty boys usually are. Jesus, that jawline was genuinely strong looking.

"Then what are you interested in, Mr. No Name?" I asked, jerking my eyes up to meet his. Dark brown, determined, a hint of warmth lurking in the depths. I was going to need to find somewhere else to look.

"It's Greg," he said, "and I'm interested in why you won't be a hero. Well, also sort of interested in why you're not a villain. You've got the prickly personality."

"I just told you, I don't want to."

"Want to what?"

"Be one. Either. Just don't want to."

"There has to be more to it," he insisted.

"Nope."

He sat back in his chair, one hand on his cup, the other resting on the table, which gave me the opportunity to follow the lines of muscle up his arm. What? Strong forearms and biceps are hot. As long as the dude doesn't end up looking like Popeye. I flicked my eyes back to his face.

"I don't think that's all there is," he said.

"Maybe I just don't want to get shot," I said.

"Don't believe it. I mean, I do believe it. That you don't want to get shot. It hurts."

"You've been shot?"

"Yeah, well, kind of."

"Kind of?"

"It was a rocket launcher."

I threw my hands up. "See, that shit right there. I don't have invincibility! Jesus Christ, how many powers do you have? Why are you guys harassing someone who only has one?"

He leaned forward. "Because you're underutilizing it. And you're a serious threat unless you're on the right side."

I laughed. "You can't be serious. I use it to make people rethink their stupid-ass decisions. And occasionally murder themselves. There's no way I'm as powerful as that."

"Yeah? What about the high school party?"

I paled. "That was different. There were drugs involved. I can't do anything like that normally, it's all concentrated on a single person." Which wasn't entirely true. There's a bit of a bystander effect. A feeling of unease in the air that everyone can sense. They don't start ripping at themselves and screaming unless I'm focused on them. But he interrupted me before I could explain any of that, and I probably wouldn't have told him the whole truth anyway.

"No," he said. "I read the file they've got on you. All the drugs did was lower your inhibitions. You're dangerous, and you're one bad romance away from—"

"Excuse me? One bad romance?"

"Yes, one tragedy or betrayal and you'll end up down a road—"

"Okay," I said, standing up. "Conversation over. You're

being ridiculous, Greg. A bad break up is not going to turn me into some kind of rampaging psychopath. Keep your promise and keep the others from pissing me off."

I stalked out. And then swore, because I forgot my coffee and there was no fucking way I was going back in there to get it.

CHAPTER TWO

Next morning, I was back in customer service. I mean, that's literally all they have me do. Stand there, help with returns and pick-ups. Sometimes I get to listen to people complain about the gift registry. But today none of my coworkers would talk to me. Apparently after taking a couple days off to recover, Lauren had told everyone about how I told her now ex-boyfriend to go ahead and shoot her. So, guess who's the pariah? Hint: it's not Lauren.

And of course, despite it being the weekend, the store was dead. Word probably got out about the "attempted shooting," so I bet shoppers will avoid this store for a couple weeks before they forget all about it. It felt like my coworkers were actively trying not to send the few people who were there my way just so I wouldn't have anyone to talk to.

Joke's on them, best workday ever. A better punishment would've been to send every little problem my way. But I made sure to loudly complain about being bored and lonely just in case they caught on, and apparently that's what they wanted to hear. You'd think they'd realize I'm not a people person. But nope. Idiots.

So yeah, it was going well until Greg came in. I saw him come through the doors, doing the "I'm a cool dude" brush back of his hair. Then he looked around and headed straight to me.

"Hey," he said.

"What are you doing here?"

"I came to talk to you."

"I thought you said you guys would stop coming to talk to me?"

"I said I would convince the others to stop harassing you. Not that I wouldn't come talk to you myself."

I scowled at him. "Well, you can go now because I'm on the clock, and I'll get in trouble if I'm standing here chit-chatting."

"Okay, well, how about you help me while we chit chat?"

"Sure, you got a return or a pickup?"

"Um, no."

"Oh well! Can't help you then! Maybe talk to one of the guys on the floor and they can help you find what you're looking for," I told him cheerfully.

"But I want you to help me," he said earnestly.

"Look," I said, "as cute as you think you're being, I don't want or need your attention. I'm doing just fine on my own."

He eyed me silently for a moment. "Are you?" he asked.

"Yuppers."

"Okay, hard way then. I want to speak to your manager."

I stared at him, bemused. "I'm sorry, what?"

"I want to speak to your manager."

"For what? Why?"

"Because you're refusing to help me."

19

"Are you trying to get me fired?" I hissed at him.

"I mean, that would be your own fault, wouldn't it? For refusing to do your job?"

I stood there glaring at him because technically he was right. "Fine," I snapped. "What are you looking for, *sir*?"

"Lightbulbs."

"Aisle 9, over near automotive. Bye, now."

"I need help finding aisle 9," he said.

"Are you-" I stopped and had to lower my voice. "Are you fucking kidding me? I can't leave the desk. Go find your stupid lightbulbs, and then come back here."

When he came back, he had three different packages. "Hey," he said, "what's the difference between 60 and 120 watt? And what about this one? It says something about being for dimmers?"

"I don't know, I'm not an electrician. I just buy the ones that look like they'll work."

He gave me a hard stare and leaned forward on the desk, which put him uncomfortably close to me. With so little distance between us, I could smell his shampoo, body wash, and also the faint scent of lemons. What? I have a sensitive nose. No one has super smell; how fucking useless would that be? Hello, I'm a human bloodhound! Okay, maybe it would have some very limited uses. Regardless, Greg was in my bubble, so I stepped back from the counter to get some space.

That was when my manager decided to show up. "Meg," he said irritably, "save the flirting for when you're off the clock."

Greg laughed. "Oh no, dude. I'm trying to figure out lightbulbs. She's not my type."

"Excuse me?" I said. I'm not sure why I was offended in that moment, but I was. Also, he's the one who asked me out, so what the fuck? And if I'm not his type, then why is he still hanging around?

"Then answer his questions and get him checked out, Meg." He left. I glared at his back.

Greg tapped the counter. "So, lightbulbs?"

"Who is your type? Tiffany?"

"No," he said. "Why? Jealous?"

"As if!" Oh yeah, I totally imitated Cher. No, I fucking didn't, but you better know what movie that's from or we can't be friends.

"You seem awfully focused on Tiffany." He sounded pleased, and I was not going to encourage that, so I switched subjects.

"Unless wherever you live has dimmer switches, you don't want these bulbs. And if you can't see in the dark, you want the 120 watt. So, I can either ring you up here or you can go flirt with one of the cashiers instead. I hear Lauren is on the rebound." I handed the package of bulbs to him. He took them, his fingers brushing mine.

"Look, Meg. Come with me."

"Come with you where?" I asked suspicious of the subject change.

"Just one mission," he begged. "I can protect you, make sure you don't get shot. Just give it a chance. How can you know you don't want to be a hero when you've never tried it? I know you don't want to be a villain."

I bristled. Not because he was wrong but because I don't like people telling me what I do or don't want. "How would you know what I want to be?"

"Just once!" he insisted. "Once, and if you absolutely don't want to do it anymore, I'll leave you alone. All of us will leave you alone. I mean, other than keeping tabs on you to make sure you don't actually turn. Which you will if—"

"Oh, for fuck's sake. I'm not going to turn. This isn't a bad romance novel, or some sort of villain trope, where the poor, misunderstood evil-doer just needs love to save her." I rolled my eyes. And who is he to judge the way I'm living my life?

"Look," he said, "my instincts on this type of stuff are pretty accurate so if you would—"

"No," I said. "Your instincts this time are wrong. Find another girl to save. And now, I would appreciate it if you would go get checked out before my manager comes back and you do actually get me fired."

∞

Their screams were still in my dreams.

I woke up in a sweat. Fucking Greg. If he would stop bringing it up maybe I wouldn't be having nightmares again. The whispers were there, just behind me. Sighing in my ears.

"Shut up," I said. They went quiet.

That's the thing about fear. It can't actually do anything to you. It's what it makes you do to yourself. But sometimes the whispers, figures and shadows like to keep me company. And nightmares bring them out more often.

I looked at the clock. 3:00 am. Great. It was going to take me forever to fall back asleep. I flopped back down onto the pillows. Then I heard the tapping at my window.

"Nevermore!" I yelled at it.

It got more insistent.

"For fuck's sake, Greg!" I yelled, throwing the blankets off me. "For the last time—" I marched up to the window.

That's when the face with red eyes loomed out of the

22

darkness and thrust itself onto the glass. "Motherfucker!" I screamed and fell backwards. It giggled, rubbing it's face back and forth. It was flat, not quite human, caught in the uncanny valley of like-but-not-like, as if its shape had begun melting away.

"Meeeeggggg," it called.

But it didn't do anything else, other than be insanely creepy that is. It continued to watch me, and then it started licking the glass with a pink tongue, long and flat like a dog's, leaving streaks of drool across the window.

"Oh gross," I said. I got up. "Look, I'm gonna tell you what I tell all the others. Go the fuck away because I'm not interested in whatever you have to offer."

"But, Meg," it said, "you know you want to. Come on, Meg. Terrify me." The voice was low and growling in pitch, and slightly muffled by the glass.

"Okay," I said, "but remember, you asked for it."

The whispers were back, the shadows elongating, stretching and rising. The figures eddying in the air, like sharks in the water. They were at the window and getting louder, going from sighs to childlike giggles. The thing grinned at me. It had very, very white fangs.

"Is that all you got, Meg?"

I frowned. "Tough customer." I pushed harder. The whispers were howling, the figures swirling, their long-fingered hands reaching through the window. They can go through glass, just not walls. What? Look, I don't make the rules, the whispers and figures are capricious. But then, they turned away from it. And came floating, swirling, reaching for *me*.

"What the fuck?!" I backed up, but they kept coming. "Oh, shit!" I said, even though logically I knew they couldn't physically hurt me. They flung themselves at me and I turned and ran. Like a fucking idiot. But I had never encountered a villain who could turn my power against me, so I guess it was understandable. I stopped halfway down the hall when I realized how stupid I was being and turned and waved a hand at them. "Begone!" Which wasn't necessary, mostly it's just dramatic effect.

They dissipated.

I went back into my room, but the face was gone.

Damn it, I was going to have to find Greg.

∞

"You just had to get an apartment that had tons of natural light, didn't you?" I muttered to myself every time I started to nod off. I spent the rest of the night camped out on the floor of my galley kitchen, sitting with my back against the cabinets. I had kept sliding into the side of the fridge where it stuck out. Not because it's a deep fridge, but because the counter and cabinets are extra shallow. I think you're underestimating how cheap my landlord is.

I hid there because it was the only section of the apartment where I had something I could hide behind out of view of the windows other than the bathroom or closets, but I didn't want to be trapped in there.

Now that the sun was up, I felt really silly.

Still, I cautiously poked my head out, checking the sliding glass doors in the living room for any sign of life.

Nothing. The balcony was empty.

Hopefully Creepy McCreeperson only comes out at night. I'm totally down with sleeping on the floor for the foreseeable future if I have to.

Or moving. I tried to remember when my lease was up.

Hadn't I just renewed the stupid thing a couple months ago?

I kicked the blankets off my feet and padded back to my room, peering around the door and at the window. There was nothing there, other than the dried streaks of drool spread across the glass.

I showered and dressed in record time. I even locked the bathroom doors, which I never do because I live alone. I didn't even lock them when Greg was here, and I barely know him. And then looked like a crazy person peeking through the crack in my door before I left my apartment. I mean, yeah, it had a peephole, but you can't see everything.

At least I had this morning off from work. I was scheduled to work the closing shift. Which was good because I needed time to find Greg and warn him about the thing from last night. Look, I said I don't want to be a hero, but I'm not so much of a jerk that I'll hide relevant villain info from them.

Seriously? That's the impression you got from me?

"Greg," I whispered into the cool morning air. He had super hearing; he should hear me if he's nearby, right? A beat passed, and I tried again, raising my voice. "Greg!"

No response.

"Gah." I hesitated there, thinking. "Hey!" I called out. "If one of you weirdos sees Greg, could you tell him I need to talk to him?"

He said they were still going to be watching me, so it was worth a try, right?

I headed to the coffee shop from Friday. Who knows, maybe Tiffany knew where he was.

She wasn't the barista at the counter when I got there. Instead, it was some gangly dude with green hair sporting a ton of facial piercings. Like, kudos to you, dude, because I could not stand having needles through my face that many times. I

25

haven't even pierced my ears. I don't have any tattoos either, because needles.

"Hey," I said to him. "When's Tiffany gonna be in, I gotta ask her a question."

"Oh, we don't tell customers when specific people are working. Liability problem."

I considered scaring him into telling me anyway. I didn't because I didn't want to hear Greg's opinion on it.

Which was weird since normally I wouldn't have cared.

Instead, I just got a large coffee to go and was headed out the door when I almost walked into someone, a tall, thin man, his limbs seeming just a tad too long. He had sallow skin, and black hair with a pronounced widow's peak. He made me think of a vampire.

No vampires aren't real. Stay on track here.

"Whoa! Watch where you're going, little lady," he said, grinning at me.

My smart-ass answer died on my lips when I saw he had very, very white teeth. And they looked kind of sharp. Instead, I skirted around him, keeping to a walk up the street. He watched me until I turned a corner.

At that point I dropped the coffee and ran for it.

∞

I tore my apartment apart looking for the business card BulletProof had left me the one time he had been sent to stop by. It had managed to get wedged under the bookcase.

44 Braxton Road was all it said. No phone number.

I pulled up the maps on my phone. Downtown. I was going to have to take the train because I live on the outskirts of Malus City in this weird mix of borough, commerce and suburbia. A little bit of searching and I realized I was going to have to deal with taking a bus to the train station, and then two bus transfers to get crisscrossed over to his section of the city. The subway would be faster, but I wasn't chancing that. What if I had to use my power with a shit-ton of people trapped in an enclosed tube with me? Jesus, I'm an asshole, not a fucking monster.

Either way, the trip could be worse, could be better. I left my apartment and headed for the bus stop at the main complex entrance. I ended up calling out sick from work on the way because I had no idea how long this was going to end up taking me. What if I ended up having to wander around downtown looking for Greg or a hero who could bring him to me? I didn't need to get fired for being a no show.

It took for-fucking-ever.

And 44 Braxton Road? A motherfucking parking lot. Who uses a parking lot as their business address? Heroes, that's who.

I swore to myself, pacing back and forth in front of the empty ticket station. I looked up and down the street. No one was really paying attention to me, so I went into the little booth, checking around for a secret button or entrance, anything that would prove this was some sort of cleverly disguised headquarters. But there was nothing. Not even a phone.

"How am I supposed to call you guys if I actually need to get a hold of you!" I kicked the wall. And immediately regretted it. "Shit!" I yelped, hopping on one foot.

"You okay, Meg?" Greg was poking his head around the door.

"Where the Hell have you been?!" I yelled at him, mostly because my foot still hurt. Not because I was concerned or something.

"Working," he said.

I huffed. "Then where is everyone else? Why would you guys give me an address for a parking lot?"

"Maybe because it's not a parking lot?"

I waved my hand at the lot behind him. "Yes, it is."

"It's not, but I'm not going to argue the semantics with you," he said. "Why are you here, Meg?" He sounded curious and hopeful.

Well, I was not going to encourage that. "Oh, I don't know," I said sarcastically, "maybe because last night I encountered some creepy asshole who can turn my power against me?"

He gave me a sharp look and then stepped into the booth with me. I hurriedly stepped backwards, bumping into the counter. There already wasn't much space, and with him in the booth there wasn't any breathing room. The sudden intimacy of how close he was made me very aware of his body, and I could feel my face flush.

"Tell me what happened." He was looking down at me, his expression troubled. He seemed oblivious to the effect he was having on me, and I needed him to back up so I could get my thoughts corralled.

I cleared my throat. "You're in my bubble."

"This isn't a joke, Meg."

"And I'm not joking! Step back, Jesus!"

He stepped back so he was standing in the doorway. I eased away from the counter. He crossed his arms, leaned against the frame, and watched me.

"Well?" he said at last. I had been distracted by the flex of his chest under his t-shirt. Jesus, Meg, stay on track! Not the time.

"Well, what?" I hedged because I didn't want him to

28

know what I had just zoned in on.

"Don't be obstinate. What happened?"

It felt silly to say it out loud. I wasn't sure how to explain it without it sounding like a total overreaction.

"Meg," he said firmly.

"Give me a second! I'm trying to figure out how to say it without it sounding fucking stupid."

He waited.

"Okay, so, last night, there was this, thing, floating outside my window. At least, I think it was floating. I'm a little fuzzy on the details. Since all I saw of it was its face."

"And?"

"It had red eyes and fangs. It licked the glass." How was I supposed to describe it? The way its face seemed too loose to fit whatever it had for a skull? The way the skin sagged and dragged against the window with the tongue?

I watched his jaw tighten. "Is that all it did?"

"No. It, it told me to scare it." At this point I was frustrated, because I couldn't figure out how to get the feeling of dread across to him without sounding like a giant chicken.

"And you listened to it?" he said exasperated.

"Of course, I did!" I snapped at him. "I figured it was another overconfident dumb ass trying to recruit me for whatever stupid plan it had in mind! I didn't realize it was going to make the fear chase me!"

He was looking me over. "Did you get hurt?"

"No."

"What happened after it turned your power against you?"

"I mean, I just released the power, and the thing left."

"And that's it?"

"Well—" And I wasn't sure what to say next, because it

29

was just a guy at a coffee shop, right? I was just going to sound paranoid.

"Well, what?"

"I mean, I think it – he – might have followed me to the coffee shop this morning."

"How do you know?"

"He had - this is going to sound stupid - he had the same teeth."

"The same teeth?" he sounded dubious.

"I said it was going to sound stupid."

"Yeah, it does."

"Oh, shut up!"

"I don't get you, Meg. You say you don't want to join us, but you come running here for help?"

"Look, jackass, I'm sorry for expecting some of you to do your damn jobs and hunt down the extra creepy ones," I fired back at him. "If he can turn my power against me, what do you think he's going to be able to do to the rest of you? But I guess fuck me for trying to warn you, right?" I started toward him; he didn't budge. "Move," I said.

"Or what?" he asked me.

"Fine. Have it your way." I hopped up onto the counter and went out the front window of the booth. Honestly, working those booths must really suck because they're totally open. What do they do during the winter?

Greg came around to follow me. "Meg, you can't leave."

"Watch me."

He stepped in front of me. "He'll be back," he told me.

"Yup, and I'm on my own apparently. So, you know, thanks for nothing." I glared at him. "You going to get out of my way?"

"No," he said.

I turned around and headed in the opposite direction. He darted back in front of me.

"Dude! Would you quit it?!"

"Make me," he said.

"What the fuck is wrong with you?"

"We need to know if all he did was turn your power back on you. Can you still use it or not?" he said, his tone brusque. "Make me."

"Are you serious right now? You're going to test me in the middle of the street, in broad daylight? You couldn't just, I don't know, ask the question like a normal person?" I asked.

No matter what he's angling, for I'm not going to be doing this down in the street where everyone can see. The heroes and villains know who I am, but not the normies. And I don't want or need the exposure. People don't need to know what I can do.

He backed down a bit. "You're right, I'm sorry. This isn't the place."

"No shit, Sherlock," I said. "Now if you'll excuse me, I apparently have to go survive on my own—"

I didn't get to finish my sentence because he charged forward, scooped me up and took off into the air. So then I was busy screaming, hiding my face and clinging to his neck. Like an idiot damsel in distress. Honestly, though, I didn't know that he wouldn't drop me, so it was a perfectly reasonable response to being kidnapped by someone who can slingshot himself straight up into the air. Shut up. And what if I had used the fear on him and we crashed? Then I'm dead.

He landed on top of a building once we were about fifty stories up. We were in the middle of downtown and surrounded by other towering skyscrapers, all steel and glass. I was surprised by the amount of heat there was as high as we were. Although I suppose I shouldn't have been, with the way the sun was reflecting off all those windows. He set me down, and I staggered away from him, grateful for the firm concrete under my feet, but also super fucking pissed.

"God damn it, Greg! What the fuck did you do that for?!" I swung at him, he dodged it.

"You don't want to hit me," he warned me.

"Why? Because it's assault? Because you fucking deserve it!"

"No, I totally deserve it, but you'll break your hand, and I don't want to hurt you, even indirectly."

I glared at him.

"Why won't you use your power on me, Meg?"

"Because that would be stupid. I do a lot of stupid things, but not that stupid."

"Well, I'm asking you to. We're up on top of a building. There's no one around to see what happens."

"Oh, you mean not from the windows or anything? Because this isn't the tallest building around."

"None of them are close enough to know what's going on."

"You know, it's super weird that you're pushing for this, and I'm not into feeding any sort of kink you have going on."

He snorted. "You wish. No, it's because I literally can't hurt myself. I'm the safest bet to test whether the red eye guy did anything more than turn your power back on you."

"Red Eye Guy? Is that really what we're going to be calling him?"

"If you come up with something better, we can always change it."

"Nope, it'll be stuck by that point."

"You're procrastinating," he told me.

"Fine," I said, the warning in my voice. "Have it your way." And I reached for them. The whispers came sighing in my ears, the light pressure of the figures' fingers sliding across my neck, shadows pooling at my feet. I told them to go after him.

They did, the shadows, whispers and figures converging on him, and for a moment, nothing happened, and then he screamed. Greg dropped to his knees clutching his head and screaming, and in a panic, I screamed at them to leave.

And they were gone.

I hesitated, steps away from him, where he knelt on the gravel, panting. I felt guilty, watching him. The silence stretched on before he finally got to his feet. He wouldn't look at me. That made me feel worse.

I don't like feeling worse than guilty.

"You asked me to do it," I said defensively.

"Right," he said. "Let's not repeat that experience."

I bristled. "I tried to tell you—"

"I know what you tried to tell me," he snapped. The fact that I made him angry made me feel smug. And then guilty again. Damn it. Wrong direction.

He rolled his shoulders back, stretching his neck side to side. "Okay," he said, "so now we know, your power is fine."

I was silent.

He started toward the edge of the roof.

"Wait!" I yelled. "Where are you going? How am I supposed to get down from here?"

"I have to go tell the others about Red Eye," he said, "and the stairs are through there." He pointed at a door set in one of the corners of the roof behind me.

"You're going to make me take the stairs after you dragged me all the way up here?"

"I thought you wouldn't be caught dead with me flying you around?"

I grimaced. "Yeah, but that was—"

"Before it was inconvenient for you?"

"Wow," I said. "Way to be a dick and rub it in. I'm not the one who made it inconvenient for me."

He stepped up to me, looking down into my face. He was really tall; I practically had to crane my neck all the way back to look up at him. Or, you know, I'm kind of short. "Step onto my feet," he said, his voice husky, "and then hold on."

"Oh no you fucking don't. I'm taking the stairs. Bye!" And I spun on my heel and headed for the door.

CHAPTER THREE

Fifty stories is a long way down, by the way. I was really regretting taking that choice before too long. Then there was the minor problem that I probably wasn't supposed to be in this building. Which is exactly why I didn't just go looking for the elevator. Also, elevators are essentially sliding death traps. I prefer to avoid them entirely anyway.

Also, who the fuck forgot to lock the door to the roof? It was Jerry, wasn't it?

What do you mean you don't watch *Rick and Morty*? Do you do anything fun? Jesus, just forget it.

But I did manage to make it down and out to the street without attracting too much attention. I guess the office workers just figured I was a temp or an intern. Wouldn't it be nice to be able to go through life without any sort of concern as to who that random stranger is?

Regardless, I got out the front door, and Greg was waiting for me.

"What the Hell, Greg?"

"I just wanted to make sure you got down okay."

"You run kind of hot and cold there, anyone ever tell

you that?" I was trying to hurry up the street because now I needed to get back to my apartment. One train, three buses, minimum.

"Not really," he said.

"Hmm. First time for everything. Aren't you supposed to be, like, alerting people or something?"

He waggled his phone at me. "All I had to do was place a few calls."

I glared at him. "Stop trying to manipulate me. Acting like you're gonna just leave me up there and then trying to make it romantic or something." His lips twitched, and I narrowed my eyes further.

He kept pace with me. "Where are you going?" Apparently he was going to just skip right by whatever I had said that he found entertaining.

"Home," I said.

"Are you sure that's safe?"

I stopped to face him. "Why wouldn't it be?"

"You already said Red Eye followed you to the coffee shop. You don't think he might show up back at your place?"

"So?" I said with more bravado than I felt. Provided he stayed outside, I should be fine. I can handle being creeped out. "What's he gonna do? Stare at me through the window? I know better than to try and attack him now."

"I don't think you should go back to your apartment until we can check it out."

"And I think I'm just gonna do the opposite of whatever you want me to, so, guess we're at an impasse."

"Then I think you shouldn't come with me for your own safety."

"You know you're supposed to use reverse psychology before they know what you're trying to do, right?"

I saw his jaw clench and was perversely happy to know I was getting to him.

"Well," I said, "this is exciting and everything, but I have a real job to get to tomorrow. So, I need to go home and sleep."

"Meg," he said.

"Greg," I mocked. "That's how you sound. I can rescue myself, you know."

He stepped up to me, and I could feel the heat from his body. What was it with this guy and crowding my space? "Here," he said, handing me a card. "This is my direct line. Call me if he shows back up."

I took it. "You know I'm not going to do that, right?"

"Don't be a hero, Meg," he said, before stepping back from me and taking off.

"That's exactly what I'm trying not to be!" I yelled after him.

∞

It was dark by the time I got back to my apartment. I don't think I've ever gotten in and locked the door behind me that quickly before. "Hello?" I called out. I was greeted by only silence. It pressed on my ears in the absence of the whispers I would normally send sweeping ahead of me. I went through the entire apartment turning on lights and checking in closets and behind the shower curtain before I was satisfied. I was alone.

What? I've had my apartment broken into before. Not this one specifically, a different one. Still, it affects your overall feeling of safety even in a new place, even if you can and did murder the person who was responsible. So, checking to make sure Red Eye hadn't broken in while I was gone was the smart move.

With a sigh, I flopped down on my couch, reaching for the remote.

There was a thud against the sliding glass doors. I froze in place.

Silence.

I started to reach for the remote again.

THUD.

"Oh, fuck this." I was off the couch and crouched behind the arm of it. The light switch was above my head, and I flicked it off. It didn't help much because the light in the galley kitchen was still on, and the light coming between the upper cabinets and countertop was reflecting off the glass doors.

Again, there was silence.

"I swear to God, Greg, if you're fucking with me just to convince me I need your help, what I did to you earlier will look like child's play!" I yelled out.

THUD-THUD-THUD.

There was a splintering sound, and I peeked out from the couch. The glass had cracked, spiderwebbing out from the center of the door. Automatically, I reached for the whispers, and they came, figures swirling forward through the glass doors across the room. But then they rushed right back at me, their fingers reaching. Panicked, I let them go, and they faded. But the glass was still slowly bowing inward.

"Oh fuck, oh fuck, oh fuck." I was pulling out Greg's card, my hands shaking as I tried to dial his number. It didn't go through the first time.

The glass was groaning and creaking as something pushed on it.

The line was ringing and ringing and ringing. Doesn't this jackass answer his phone?!

"Hello?" came the voice on the other end.

"Are you on my balcony?" I hissed into the phone. "Because this isn't fucking funny."

"I'm on my way."

"Wait, don't—" The line went dead.

The glass finally shattered, scattering across the carpet.

I darted for the front door, and something big, black and red-eyed came charging after me.

I totally screamed. I know, I'm such a wuss. But you try dealing with suddenly being deprived of the defensive maneuver you've had your whole life.

It leapt at me while I was trying to get the door unlocked, and then, before it could reach me, it was like it paused in midair. It was a mix between a bear and a dog, like a Newfoundland, with gleaming white fangs and long, matted fur. But it's expression had gone from slavering to bewildered.

I heard a strangled yelp, and then it was yanked out of the air away from me, and I heard it slam into the wall of the dining room. I wasn't sure, but it sounded like it went through the wall because I'm pretty sure the neighbors on that side of the building screamed.

And then Greg was next to me. He had yanked the door out of the way, locks, hinges and all. "I've got you," he said, as he swept me up, and then we were in the air.

∞

He landed us somewhere way out of the city, in an empty field of long grass. I hadn't kept track; I was trying not to have a panic attack. He set me down, and I shoved myself away from him.

"Jesus," I gasped. "I think it was going to try to fucking eat me." I sat down because I wasn't sure my legs would support me. And then I giggled. I mean, how could it not be somewhat hysterical in that moment? The girl with the power of fear, afraid of a fucking dog.

Okay, most dogs don't have red, glowing eyes. But come on. What kind of reaction was screaming and running away?

Oh wait, that's right, I could've died.

"Are you okay?" he asked hesitantly.

"Do I look okay to you?" I giggled again.

"Not really." His tone was cautious, like he wasn't sure if I was being serious or not.

"Winner, winner, chicken dinner."

"You're hysterical," he said.

"People don't usually find me that funny," I said. "Obviously, that means I am hilarious."

"No, not hysterical as in funny. Hysterical as in having hysterics. You need to take a breath." He knelt next to me. "Like this: breathe in for a count of four, hold it - one, two, three, four - breathe out - one, two, three, four."

The world got a lot less funny that way. But at least I wasn't breaking into giggles anymore.

He patted me on the shoulder, his face next to mine. "Good news: it doesn't seem like Red Eye can adjust to surprises quickly. I think he needs a chance to get your measure first."

"How the fuck does that help me?" Obviously he already had my measure since there was no pause when my power turned back on me. "And how do we know that was him and not some sort of minion?"

"I mean, you think he would want his minion to eat you before he could carry out whatever nefarious plan it is he has?"

"You," I said sternly, "are not helping."

He brushed his hair back out of his face. He looked frustrated. "I literally just saved you from whatever that was. You could try not being sarcastic for five minutes."

"Oh, I'm sorry, Mr. Invincible Man, that I'm being sarcastic when I'm faced with the fact that I could've just fucking died!" At the face he made, I took a minute to take stock. "Oh my God, I'm just like all the other ingrates."

"Ingrates?"

"Like, does anyone ever thank you for saving them?" I demanded. "Or do they just do what I did and bitch about the fact that they just had to face their own mortality?"

"Sometimes I get the former," he said honestly.

"Why do you even do it? Why do you put up with people like me?" I would've just left my ass to fend for myself in that field.

"Someone has to do the right thing."

I bit back my snarky response to that. Because what did doing the right thing ever get someone? But I didn't think I was going to convince him of that.

"Okay, fine. So, are we sleeping in the field?" I asked. "Because I've got work tomorrow, and all my clothes are back at my apartment with that thing," I griped. "Oh shit! My neighbors! Did you actually throw that thing into their apartment?"

There wasn't much light, but we were close enough that I could see the grim look on his face. "God damn it! The wall!" he swore. "I have to go check." He started to get up.

I grabbed at his arm. "What? Don't! You want him using your powers against you?"

He gently pulled my hand off his arm. "I'll be fine."

"I'm pretty sure that's my line," I said, surging to my feet. To, I don't know, chase after him? Yeah, useless I'm sure, but he didn't move away from me. "You're going to risk him being able to, I don't know, pull you out of the air? What happens if he turns your invincibility against you? Are you just gonna, like, implode or something?" He must have heard something in my voice because he stayed there, hesitating.

"I can't stand here and do nothing while he's potentially rampaging through your apartment complex," he said adamantly.

"Yes, you absolutely can! What happens to everyone else if you die because you go off half-cocked? You already said the rest needed to look into this first!"

"I'm wasting time," he said flatly. "I'm going. Stay here, I'll be back."

He was backing up from me, and I started to follow, yelling as I went because he was not going to get away with leaving me there. "What? No! I'm not standing in a field in the middle of fucking nowhere while you go—"

He took off.

"God damn it, Greg!" I yelled at the air.

The only other sound was crickets. Grumbling, I sat back down in the grass only to realize it was wet, which meant my jeans were also wet. And cold.

Because I'm a stubborn asshole, I sat there and shivered.

It didn't take long for Greg to get back. I scrambled to my feet when he landed a couple yards away from me. He didn't say anything. I stood there silently because I knew it was bad news. After several minutes, though, I couldn't stand the suspense.

"Greg? Greg!" I said. He looked at me. "What

42

happened?"

"He wasn't there," he said.

"And?"

"Your neighbors are dead."

"Fuck," I said. I had kind of liked them. They tended to keep to themselves and were pretty quiet. Knowing my luck, I was now going to get the kind of asshole who plays Norwegian Death Metal at 2:00 am.

"He left you a message." Greg sounded angry.

"Like, on paper? You didn't touch it, did you?"

"No, not on paper."

"Well, how then?" I asked, getting irritated. "What did it say?"

He scrubbed at his face. "I don't know that I should tell you that."

"You know I'll just go back to my apartment and take a look for myself if you don't, right?"

"I can stop you."

I think I sounded like a boiling tea kettle. "Don't you even try it. I will disable you so fucking badly you will be screaming for weeks. I swear to God, Greg."

We stood facing each other. In the dark, all I could see was the vague shape of him. The whispers were at my back, sibilant and vicious, and all they needed was for him to be in their reach.

"Can the fear move faster than I can?" he asked. "Because I know you won't try that in the air."

"Don't you fucking dare," I snarled through gritted teeth. Because he was right, and I knew it. If he got me into the air quickly enough, I would stop, and he would have won. That battle, at least. Because then he was going to have to deal with me once we landed.

"Meg," he sounded tired. "Can you just accept that I'm trying to protect you?"

"Then work with me instead of trying to shove me around like a chess piece!" Even if I didn't doubt the sincerity I heard in his voice at that moment, I don't respond well to people trying to make me do anything. So, I shouted it at him.

He was silent for a long moment.

"Please," he said finally, "come here."

I hesitated, but it was the please that made me respond. "Why?" I asked suspiciously.

He sighed. "I'll take you back to your apartment. I'll show you the message. You need clothes anyway." I was on the verge of agreeing before his next sentence. "But," he said, "and this is a big but – you need to come back to my place after, where it's secure."

"No. No way," I said. "I can get a room at a hotel. I mean, a cheap one, but there's no way I am staying at your place."

I was pretty sure the noise he made was him grinding his teeth. I wanted to ask if his teeth were included in the invincible part or if he was gonna need to go see a dentist from wearing them down so badly.

"Meg. He can find you in a hotel."

"We don't know that he wants to find me *that* badly," I said.

"Yes, he does. You need to trust me on this." He sounded worried or desperate. Maybe it was both.

At this point I was positive that he was nearing the end of his patience, and after my latest experience with Red Eye, I wasn't entirely confident in my ability to rescue myself. I had to grudgingly admit that I needed his help.

But because I can't help being uncooperative, I had a

demand.

"Okay, on one condition." He let out an exasperated sigh. "Deal with it," I snapped. "One condition. I see the message first and *then* I decide if I'm going with you or getting a hotel."

"Okay," he said.

"Okay?"

"Yes, okay. Now will you come here?"

I stepped up to him, and he wrapped an arm around my waist, pulling me up against him. "Step onto my feet. And hold on," he warned me.

"Don't try and get handsy with me."

He chuckled.

"I'm serious, Greg."

"I wouldn't dream of it."

I scowled up at him. Even though I was fairly sure he couldn't clearly see the expression on my face, I was going to scowl anyway.

"Are you holding on?" he asked, his voice low.

"Stop fucking flirting with me. I'm pretty sure you can tell I am." Totally inappropriate timing, Greg.

And then we were in the air, my face buried in his chest.

Okay, yes, I'm afraid of heights. Shut up.

∞

The message was written on the wall, in blood. And since he hadn't been carrying a bucket with him - because dog shape, no hands - I could only assume he used what he found on site. Which meant that was my neighbor's blood smeared across the living room wall.

"Come play with me, Meg," it read.

"Wow," I said. "And I thought I was melodramatic."

Greg made a noise behind me.

"Stop grinding your teeth. I can't imagine what your dental bills will be." I moved past him, back through the hole in the wall between the two apartments. He followed me. I paused to look around. My apartment was a mess. Glass was strewn across the living room; my front door was lodged in the fridge in the kitchen. I wasn't even entirely sure how that was possible. It looked like it might have hit a couple corners on the way there because pieces were missing from the walls and there were bits of drywall strewn around.

"Definitely not getting my security deposit back," I said.

Greg made another noise.

I shot him a look. "Chill, dude."

"Chill?" he said, voice strangled. "How can you be so blasé about this?"

I waved a hand at the apartment. "No bad guys right now. So, we're fine, right?"

He glared at me.

"You know, I'm beginning to think you don't share my opinions of things." I headed into my bedroom, and he followed me. "Uh-uh," I said. "What do you think you're doing?"

"Keeping tabs on you in case there are bad guys."

I snorted. "Uh-huh. Sure, that's it." I opened my closet pulling out my little roller suitcase. I set it on the bed and popped it open.

"You're packing," he said, wary.

"Yup. You knew I wasn't going to stay here." I checked the time. "And I'm gonna need to sleep somewhere. How is it already 1:00? Damn it, I have work tomorrow." I was pulling clothes indiscriminately out of the dresser. Underwear, shirts, bras, socks, jeans. I just piled them on in there. I found my pajamas on the bathroom floor where I had left them. Gross. I pulled out a clean pair for the suitcase. Tossed in soap, shampoo, conditioner. Razor. Wide tooth comb, curly hair care, duh. No makeup, though, I'm not going to be getting all gussied up. Just because I keep having ideas doesn't mean Greg needs to think the same thing. I closed the suitcase and locked it.

I looked Greg over. "How much weight can you carry at once? Do we need to take a bus?"

He looked surprised. "You're coming with me?"

"Yes?" I said. "I'm argumentative, not stupid. Can you carry me and the suitcase at the same time or what?"

"You're going to let me fly you?"

"Look, I thought you were in a hurry?"

"I am, but I'm looking for your angle."

"My angle is not dying." I pointed in the general direction of the message. "That sounds an awful lot like dying would be involved."

He nodded. "Yes, it does." He scooped me up before I could protest, grabbed the suitcase with his free hand and tucked it under his arm. "Put your arm around my neck."

I complied, but only because I wouldn't have been able to get out of his grip anyway. "You could've waited until we were outside," I said as he headed out the remnants of the front door.

"Could've. But I didn't."

We didn't talk on the flight there. Because I was busy, you know, not panicking or anything.

CHAPTER FOUR

We landed on the roof of a building downtown, gravel crunching under his feet. Lights from some of the apartments in the other high-rises around us were still on. A glimpse into how other people lived if I wanted to stay there with him and watch them for long enough. Which I didn't. Greg set me down and then used a keycard to unlock the door to the stairs down. He looked back at me.

"You coming?"

"Seriously? This is your secure location?"

He huffed. "Unlike *your* apartment, *mine* is reinforced. He's not getting in here."

I stepped past him through the doorway. The stairwell was well-lit but otherwise nondescript. Just like any other concrete, walled structure. He closed the door behind us, and I heard the whir-click as it locked itself. It sounded very solid and heavy. He slid around me and started down the stairs, still carrying my suitcase.

"I can carry that," I said, reluctant to take any further help.

"I've got it," he said.

"What if I don't want you to have it?" I snapped.

He turned to look back at me. With him on the lower steps, we were almost eye to eye.

"Me carrying your suitcase isn't going to make any kind of statement about your level of independence, Meg. You can accept help without thinking there's some kind of toll you're going to have pay later."

I clenched my jaw but didn't refute what he said. He continued down the stairs. Because at this point my choice was sleep in a stairwell or follow him, I followed him.

A few floors down he paused to unlock a door into a hallway that was just as nondescript as the stairwell. It too made a very solid thunk when he closed it behind me. Again, it locked itself. I eyed it.

"You weren't kidding about the security."

"Yeah, well, the villains aren't showing up here to try and recruit us." He trotted down toward the end of the hall before unlocking a door with the number 4 on it. He hit the light switches just inside, and then stepped back so I could move past him. He closed the door behind me. Another THUNK.

"There are other heroes here?" I asked.

"Yup," he said.

Well, that was informative. No really, it was. Because there's only one building in Malus City that would have this kind of security and multiple heroes.

Stepping in, I took a look around. His apartment was a LOT bigger than mine. And a studio, so bed, living, dining, kitchen all in one giant-ass room. There was also a small loft above that looked like it was being used as an office, and only a single door that I assumed led to a bathroom.

Well, hopefully it was the bathroom. It didn't look like the tub and toilet were in this room. So, at least I wasn't going to have to shower in front of him.

Look, I've heard about some of the conditions of the downtown apartments. Tubs right there, in the living room.

He set my suitcase down next to the couch. "The couch up in the loft is a fold out. I'll get it set up for you."

"Thanks," I said grudgingly. At least he wasn't expecting me to sleep in the living room. Oh, I'm sorry? Were you expecting some enthusiastic show of gratitude from me? Have you heard a single word I've said?

He headed up the circular staircase while I wandered around the downstairs, taking in the furniture and state-of-the-art entertainment system. A dark couch, pillows in the corners. A coffee table and TV stand in walnut. Heavyset and masculine with clean lines, the furniture looked incredibly sturdy. TV, speakers center, right and left on the stand, and I was willing to bet there would be mid and rear speakers that were well hidden somewhere, somehow. I kept my face averted from the bed set at my left over near the loft.

"Wow, the hero business must pay *really* well," I called up to him.

"It does when you're government employed," he said. I could hear the phumpf of cushions being tossed onto the floor and the groan of springs as he pulled the bed portion of the couch out.

"Some of you are - what, freelance?"

"Vigilante is." Rustling noises of sheets. "He said something to me once about not wanting to be beholden to a bunch of corrupt politicians."

"He's probably got the right idea," I muttered.

"You know I can hear you, right?"

I ran a finger down the length of the dining room table and didn't answer him. It didn't seem to match the aesthetics of the rest of the pieces. It was strangely delicate in comparison to the living room set, even to the stools I could see hidden under the island counter in the kitchen.

"It's teak." He was looking over the railing at me.

"Expensive taste for a superhero."

He snorted. "I didn't pick it out, and now I can't get anyone to take the stupid thing."

"You bought a table you didn't want? And can't get rid of it why? Charging too much?"

"I don't want to discuss it."

Well, that was intriguing. "Why not?" I demanded.

He came down the stairs and headed into the kitchen. He pulled a pitcher of water out of the fridge. There were slices of lemon in it.

"You want anything to drink? Or eat?"

I sat down on one of the stools at the kitchen island while he reached into a cabinet. "Nope. I want to know about this table. And why you're avoiding the subject."

He poured himself a glass of the lemon water and set the pitcher back in the fridge. He took his glass and sat down on the couch.

"Oh!" I said, swiveling around on the stool to face him. "So, it's not okay for me to be all obstinate and moody, but you get to do it?"

"Ex-girlfriend," he finally grunted. "She joined the other side."

"Well that explains a lot. You're projecting. Who dumped who?"

He glared at me. "I am not projecting."

"Uh huh," I said wisely, just to irritate him. "Whatever you say, dude." I hopped off the stool. "Well, I'm going to bed because I've got to go to work in the morning, unlike some people."

"No, you don't."

"Excuse me?"

"You're not going to work tomorrow."

"Um, yes, I am. Because also unlike some people I have to show up to a specific place at a specific time for a specific number of hours to get paid."

"You," he said, motioning at the walls with the glass in his hand, "are staying right here with about three feet of reinforced concrete between you and Red Eye."

I pointed at the window. "And what are those made of?"

"Not glass," he said. "He's not getting through those either."

I stood there, trying to think of an argument. Because I realized I had basically just trapped myself. I was in the building full of heroes. As in the one that belongs to a branch of the military. The very same people who keep trying to convince me to contract my life away. I wasn't getting out without going through Greg.

"The others all know you're here," he said, almost as if he had read my mind.

Which meant I was right. If I wanted to get out, I had an unspecified number of people who would try to stop me. And I didn't care what he had told me about underutilizing my power. Trying to see how far it would stretch in the current circumstances didn't seem like the smartest move.

"Just call in sick tomorrow," he suggested. "Or tell them someone died. It's technically the truth."

"Exactly how many days am I calling in sick for? I don't really get bereavement leave."

"As many as it takes."

He must have seen the look on my face because his tone gentled.

"Take a breath; I'll make sure you don't lose your home. And don't worry about the bills, they'll get paid."

That pissed me off. "I'm not a fucking charity case. You can take your government sponsorship and shove it!" I shouted at him as I stormed up the stairs to the loft.

There is nothing less satisfying than not having a door to slam shut in someone's face when you want to make a point.

∞

The alarm on my phone was going off, the annoying singsong beeping gratingly cheerful. I pulled the pillow over my head but could still hear it.

Then, silence. I immediately sat up.

Greg held my phone out to me. "Here. I turned it off, I thought you might've wanted to sleep in."

I snatched it from him. "No, because apparently I have to call in sick today."

He stood there watching me.

"Go away," I said.

He didn't move.

"I'm getting really tired of telling you to leave me alone," I snapped at him. "What're you waiting for?"

"I'm headed out to pick up breakfast. I was going to ask you what you wanted."

"What? Too rich to cook for yourself?" I sneered at him.

Damn was I in a bitchy mood. What? You already knew I wasn't a morning person. Don't give me that look.

To his credit, he didn't rise to the bait. He ignored my

attitude. "I'll be back. The door is going to lock behind me, so you won't be able to leave." He turned around and headed down the stairs and out the door. I heard the whir and click as it locked, just like he said it would.

And that gave me an idea.

I called my manager to tell him my apartment had been broken into and my neighbors murdered on the same night, so I was staying out of town with a friend until the police got back to me about whether I was the actual target or it was just coincidence. Because it was kind of the truth, and it would buy me more time than just being sick would.

He didn't sound very concerned about me. The only thing he made sure to tell me was that any time I was taking off was unpaid. Which, duh. And then he hung up on me. Asshole. I glared at my phone. Maybe I should just quit. Not like that job is that great anyway.

And then I had nothing to do but wait. I prowled around Greg's apartment and checked the windows. They certainly looked thick, and there was no way to open them. Why would you give the guy who can fly an apartment without a way to just jump out a window? Not even a balcony.

Which, honestly, does he realize he's living in a cage? What if his bosses decide they need to keep him contained and change the code on his door? If all the doors are coded like that, then couldn't they just exterminate the heroes they decide are more trouble than they're worth?

It's not like it hasn't happened before. Back in the 1980's a government decided the heroes they were employing had become an issue.

I'm not arguing that they might not have been right, but a lot of people died when they decided to take them down because unlike our good ol' US of A, they did not have this kind of security to trap people with.

I know what you're thinking, and no, it wasn't Russia, it wasn't China, it wasn't even North Korea.

It was France.

I don't want anyone having that kind of jurisdiction over me.

The thought was unsettling and made me more determined. I needed to be gone before someone decided I was a problem. Greg could do what he wanted, but I wouldn't want to work for someone who keeps those kinds of contingency plans in place.

The whir-click was my first clue that Greg was back. He shouldered the door open, carrying a drink tray and a paper bag. He set them down on the island without looking at me. He pulled one of the cups out of the tray and set it down in front of a stool. "Large coffee, black." He tossed something wrapped in paper he had dug out of the bag down next to it. "Egg and cheese croissant. I wasn't sure what you would want."

I sat at the island, head down. "Thanks," I said.

"You're welcome," he said stiffly, before taking his drink and sandwich over to the couch.

There was a lot of awkward silence while we ate. I mean, he didn't even turn on the TV for the news or anything, and I spent most of it facing away from him. It made my back itch because I didn't know if he ever looked in my direction.

I didn't know how long I was going to have to sit here with him before I could put my plan into action, and I'm not exactly the patient kind of person. I needed him to take a nap or something.

He came around to throw his trash away and finally actually looked at me. "I can hear your heart beating. What are you planning, Meg?"

I choked on my coffee. And sputtered while I coughed it up.

He was next to me with a towel, one warm hand on my back, and for a moment I felt bad about what I had planned. Well, more about the not pointing out the prison he was living in and recommending he get away while he could. Less about the fact that once I had a chance I was getting out while the getting was good.

"Nothing," I wheezed out. "Jesus."

"Are you alright?"

"Fine." I coughed a bit more. "Don't do that."

"Do what?" His hand was still on my back, and his touch was disconcerting. I shifted away from him because I didn't know what answer I wanted to give him. He pulled his hand away. "Sorry," he said.

"You really shouldn't tell a girl you can hear her heartbeat from across a counter, Greg. It doesn't have the effect you think it does."

He just watched me.

"Staring does not help your case."

"Meg," he said, his tone serious, "I don't know why you're nervous, but I can tell you are. Don't do anything stupid."

"I try to avoid doing stupid things at all costs," I said, straight-faced.

I couldn't be sure, but I think he was having to fight not to grin at me. Which was good, I needed him disarmed.

Except then he leaned onto the counter so that his face was level with mine. "I'm not falling for that," he said, and then he walked away from me.

Damn it.

∞

He had locked me in again, saying he had a meeting. I
tried the door this time just in case he was lying. It was
definitely locked.

Being trapped makes me anxious. Not being told I was
for all intents and purposes a prisoner even more so. I'm not
an anarchist, but I do have serious issues with someone having
this kind of control over me.

I went through his closet looking for a book bag. I
didn't want to just abandon all my stuff here, and I'm not made
of money. I can't just go around buying new clothes all the
time. And I wanted to make sure my hands were going to be
free instead of lugging around a suitcase.

Luckily, I found one buried in the back.

Most of what was in his closet was a couple hoodies, his
jeans - can you believe the guy hangs his jeans up? - some polos
that still had tags, and some shoeboxes. When I moved one, I
could hear the contents shifting. It sounded like photos or
maybe papers. I hesitated because I'm nosy, but how much of a
line did I want to cross? I set it aside, and that was when I
found his hero outfit, crumpled in a back corner. He hadn't
worn it on any of the occasions I had seen him, even when he
was supposed to be working. I pulled it out and giggled. Well, I
couldn't blame him, I wouldn't wear it either. They had given
him a cape. The color wasn't completely horrible, muted greys,
but the cape was copper. I giggled again before shoving it back
into the corner I had found it in and backing out of the closet
with the bookbag clutched to my chest. I made sure the
mystery shoebox was back in there, too, before I shut the door.

I put a couple changes of clothes down in the bottom of
the bookbag and a bag of toiletries on top of those. Then I hid

it under the couch in the living room.

And now I was stuck biding my time again. I tried to watch TV, but I wasn't sure which remote went to what. I considered hiding them just to be petty. I didn't because I didn't want to explain where the remotes went if he decided to watch TV while I was still there.

Instead, I spent a lot of time pacing, the whispers, figures and shadows curling around me. I needed the noise the whispers made; otherwise it was too quiet and nerve-wracking here. I went through his fridge. There was a lot of healthy stuff. Mostly produce. A carton of eggs. The pitcher of lemon water. No soda, no beer, no meat products. It bothered me that it looked like he didn't have any vices. Other than constantly getting in my personal space. The whispers faded when I started looking through the cabinets. I think they were bored. But I continued poking through his things. The pantry was also mostly healthy things: flaxseed, protein powders. No chips or other snack foods. Oh wait, there were deluxe mixed nuts. Not even close to the same thing. No sugar or maple syrup either, which was just plain weird to me.

"Jesus, what is he? A saint?" I muttered to myself pulling my head back out of the pantry.

"Not even close to one," he said right next to me.

"Motherfucker!" I gasped, banging my back into the cabinets as I jumped away from him. "Don't do that!" How did he manage to sneak in like that in the first place? You would think I would've heard the door, even if he had sneaky ninja feet. If he had more than the four powers I knew about I was going to need a moment. Get your mind out of the gutter, not like that!

"Why are you going through my things?"

"I was bored," I said.

"Bored?" he asked.

"You left me locked in with nothing to do."

"So, it's okay for you to just go through my stuff? Why the pantry? There's more interesting places to look." He didn't sound mad, though, his voice had gone husky again.

"I was looking for lunch," I snapped at him, going for anger because I was still not going to encourage that. "How do you not even have sandwich meats?"

"I deal with enough blood during the day. I don't want to eat it, too," he said.

"You have eggs," I said slowly.

"Yeah, eggs aren't fertilized. You don't have to kill something to get food out of them."

"So, you're a vegetarian?" I asked, trying to remember if they were allowed to eat eggs or not.

He shrugged. "If you have to have a label for it, sure."

"But is that the right label for it?"

He shrugged again.

"Right. So, what would you normally do for lunch?" I was getting frustrated with his non-answers and needed to move past the lack of label. Look, it takes me a minute to get over things. The label or lack thereof isn't actually important; I'm just stubborn and will argue semantics until I'm blue in the face.

"Salad," he said, pulling things out of the fridge. There was a bowl of boiled eggs I hadn't noticed on my perusal that he set on the counter. I watched him as he peeled, chopped, and tossed things into a large glass bowl. He ignored me. When he was done, he used tongs to put a bunch of it into a small bowl and slid it over to me with a fork. He set down vinegar and oil dispensers on the counter. "There. Lunch."

I poked it with my fork. It was definitely colorful.

"Meg," he sounded torn between amusement and irritation, "it's a salad. It's not going to bite you. And you might want to put some dressing on it; otherwise it's going to taste mostly green."

I followed his advice and then tasted it. I felt my eyes widen. "It's good," I said around a mouthful. "I thought salad was supposed to be boring."

"It is if all you put in it is lettuce." He took the large bowl he had used to make the salad to the couch. I turned so I was still facing him.

"Is there a reason you're sitting across the room from me?"

"I thought you wanted your space," he told me.

Well, yes, but only when it didn't feel like he was avoiding me. But I couldn't tell him that. So instead, we both suffered through the awkward-while-eating silence. I mean, I assumed he was suffering, since I was having a hard time not making wise-ass comments. I hate silence. You wouldn't think someone like me would, but I often have the whispers and figures with me when I'm alone. So it's almost never truly silent around me.

He came around and collected my bowl when we were both done. I watched him as he washed the dishes, and he ignored me some more. He had set them aside in the dishrack before I spoke up.

"So, what exactly is happening right now?

He leaned back, hands resting on the edge of the sink behind him. "Happening with what?"

"Don't be all coy with me. With the thing. How much longer am I stuck here? Also, am I gonna be stuck here by myself all the time? Because you're gonna need to show me how to work the TV if I am."

He crossed his arms. "We can't find him. So, I don't know."

I took a breath. "Have you tried the coffee shop?"

He didn't look amused. "We have people keeping an eye on anywhere you would go. Your apartment, nearby hotels, your place of employment, the grocery store you use, your pharmacy, even your doctor's office. He hasn't shown up."

"That's kind of creepy that you guys keep tabs that closely on me."

"We keep tabs like that on almost anyone who's undecided."

"Thought you said I was special," I said.

He sighed. "Can you not - just for five minutes - can you not be a smart ass?"

"Nope. Sorry, it's my default mode."

"You don't sound very sorry."

"Because I'm not?" I mean, I wasn't. So at least he was getting honesty?

He shook his head. "Okay, have it your way. I'll be back later."

"Now where are you going?"

"I have a separate mission. Unlike what you seem to think, babysitting you is not my primary." And he left.

"Fine! Be that way. I don't need you for entertainment!" I yelled at the door after it closed behind him. What? I needed to get the last word in. And unlike me, he didn't seem like the type to come back in just so he can win the argument. I'm fine with winning by default. He heard, though, right?

∞

It was after midnight before he got back. I knew because I had curled up on the pull-out couch, occasionally nodding off while I waited. I mean, he had to come home and sleep at some point, right? No one can just go all the time.

I heard the door open and close, quiet footsteps coming in. An exasperated sigh.

"I know you're awake, Meg. I can tell by your breathing."

I didn't answer him. I wanted him to think I was sitting up there stewing and pouting rather than plotting.

Another exasperated sigh. "Fine. Be that way. I'm going to bed. Try to behave yourself."

I waited until the sounds downstairs stopped. And then I waited some more, watching the time pass on my phone screen. I realized I had forgotten to grab my charger from the apartment. Damn it, I was going to have to get another one. I didn't dare go home to try and retrieve mine. Even if I could make it that far out of the city proper in the middle of the night.

It was two in the morning before I slowly uncurled and climbed off the couch. I padded down the stairs, shoes in my hands. I paused at the bottom, waiting and listening. Nothing. I set the shoes down by the couch and eased toward his bed. I wanted to check the nightstands first.

His keycard was sitting right there. Ha, you're too trusting, Greg. Although, honestly, it was probably more out of habit than the assumption that I wouldn't do anything truly stupid or sneaky. Sucks for you, Greg. I do both regularly just to piss people off. I know what I told him earlier. I lied, duh.

Carefully, I pulled it off, trying not to wince at the slight scraping noise. Then I froze. No movement. Just his quiet breathing. Oh, thank God I got stuck with a deep sleeper of a hero. Guess REM trumps super hearing. I snuck back over to the couch and wiggled the bookbag out from under it. I swung it onto my back and picked my shoes up. Padded quietly in stocking feet to the door. I felt the keycard over with my fingers. Damn it, which side needed to slide through? I took a guess. Nothing happened. I turned it over. It beeped and I quickly swung the handle down, cracking the door so it wouldn't lock itself. Then I waited. Nothing, it was still quiet.

That door was fucking heavy. I got it open enough that I could slide myself and the bookbag through, and then basically had to lean against it to keep it from slamming shut. I heard it whir and click.

"Ha," I breathed out quietly. "I bet it'll take even you some time to get out that door." If he could get out at all. I wasn't sure what scale of strength it was he had.

I got my shoes on and ran for the stairwell. Slid the keycard through, heard it beep with relief. I dragged it open and then ignored it slamming shut behind me because I was busy racing down the stairs as fast as I could without falling. And yes, once again I didn't bother looking for an elevator. Would it have been faster than the stairs? Yes. Was it the perfect place to get myself trapped again? Also, yes. So, don't @ me about fucking elevators.

The numbers of the floors were flashing by, and I was getting nervous because we were pretty high up, and I knew how long it had taken me to climb down just fifty stories before. Although I hadn't been hell bent on escaping that time. And it was awfully quiet. Where were the leagues of heroes who knew I was here?

One of the doors below me slammed open. Right on cue, I thought grimly, and as he stepped into the stairwell yelling at me to stop, I hit him with the fear. He fell back against the door screaming and clawing at his arms.

"Sorry! Sorry!" I called as I raced past him, pulling my power back. I honestly didn't want to hurt him. I left him there at the door panting and bleeding. But he was alive and would recover.

This time I kept the whispers with me and sent the shadows sweeping along ahead of me, the figures running long-fingered hands down the walls and across the doors. Several times I heard the locks beep, but the doors didn't open as whomever was on the other side rethought their decision to stop me.

The whispers were howling in my ears when I reached the bottom of the stairs. I had to drag the door open, and the guards in the lobby just watched me while the figures swirled around me. I headed towards the front doors, and the guards stumbled back away from me. The fear was so thick in the air I could almost taste it.

"Stop," one of them demanded his voice shaking.

I looked at him. "Make me." He paled and fell back behind the other one. The second one ran toward a desk. "No, you don't," I said. The figures rushed him. He screamed, waving his hands wildly around his head as he batted at things he couldn't touch, and as I pulled them back, he fell to the ground whimpering. I went out the front doors, and I was on the street. I was free.

I ran.

CHAPTER FIVE

Buses don't run at two in the morning by the way.
Stores and internet cafes aren't open.

But you know what is open?

Night clubs. Bars. Strip joints.

I went searching for the seediest spot I could find.
Because I was going to hide out there until things started to
open up. I needed to get a new phone charger and to hit up an
internet café. Which, why are they closed at 2:00 am? Don't
they know people need to be able to buy tickets for buses going
out of town?

The hole in the wall I found was definitely full of the
dregs of society. It and they smelled of cheap beer and gin. The
walls were covered in paneling, the bar was chipped, and the
vinyl on the booths was cracked, their stuffing poking through.
Some of the guys were eyeing me, but when they heard the
whispers following me, they averted their gaze. Only the stupid
or truly desperate would've tried to get anywhere near me. And
if they did, they would die. Because unlike most people with
powers, mine had always been willing to act without my direct
input. My parents never had to worry about what my babysitter

would do. They had to be more worried about what could happen to the sitter.

I disappeared into the depths of a corner booth where I would be safe enough until morning. I told the whispers to watch over me. And they agreed, because they wanted more blood; I could feel the pressure of their fingers sliding across my skin. I ignored it, curled up as tightly as I could in the corner, and dozed off.

No one bothered me until morning when the whispers giggled to me. I opened my eyes; the bartender was standing well out of arms' reach.

"You need to leave," he grunted. "We've been closed since 4:00, and now it's 8:00, and I need you to leave." Sweat was dripping down his face. Did it take him those whole four hours to build up the courage to wake me? Regardless, I needed to get moving before anyone found me, and I had slept later than I meant to.

He backed away from me as I slid toward him. I walked past him and out the door into the sun.

The streets were mostly empty.

Well, they would be in this part of town at this time of morning.

I pulled out my phone to check the maps for the closest internet café and realized I was basically carrying around a tracking device in my pocket. I hesitated, trying to decide how far off the grid I wanted to chance it.

If Red Eye found me first, I might need it for whatever chance it would give Greg or whomever else to find me, preferably before I got murdered.

Well, I couldn't just stand around in the middle of the street. That would guarantee I got found sooner rather than later. I found the internet café and started up the sidewalk, following the directions while scurrying along, glancing left and right and back over my shoulder as much as I looked ahead.

I didn't stick out that much because everyone else I saw out looked just as twitchy as I did. And then I stopped in the middle of the sidewalk. Why the fuck was I headed somewhere with internet? I could buy the ticket on my phone. Oh wait, duh, because they would let me charge my phone there. I kept going.

Jesus, all this indecision was going to get me killed. Look, I don't usually have to think on my feet like this. Normally I scare the shit out of people and go about my merry way. Cut me some slack.

I reached the café. Fortunately for me, they had plenty of extra chargers for sale. I bought one. I didn't have a choice, I had to use my debit card because I didn't have any cash. And I knew that was going to be a problem later. I got my phone plugged in, and while I was waiting, I pulled up the bus schedule.

There was one going cross country leaving at 11:00 am from the station nearest me.

Would that be far enough away from Red Eye? I just needed to stay hidden long enough for the others to be able to handle him.

I might have just made a really, really stupid choice in running from Greg's apartment. But I had never done well when others expected me to just comply without any sort of explanation.

Might be why I'm not the best fit for the job I do have. Well, might still have.

I went ahead and bought the ticket anyway. I checked the maps; it wasn't a long walk. I could wait here for a bit so my phone could charge some more.

It was then that I realized the one other customer in the store wasn't looking at his computer. He was watching me.

Oh, fuck, it was the guy from the coffee shop.

My palms sweating, I tried to discretely pull Greg's business card from where I had stashed it in my back pocket. The cardboard was slick on my fingers.

Oh my God, I could just text him from recent calls. What the fuck am I doing?

I changed tactics - sent a text with the name and address of the internet café. Then I sent him a real time location. I maxed out the number of hours it would keep relaying the information.

I looked up from my phone.

"Hello, little lady," he purred, white teeth bared in a grin, as he leaned over me.

Run, said the whispers.

They didn't have to tell me twice. I surged up out of my seat, surprising Red Eye into stumbling back. I think he thought I might be stupid enough to try hitting him with my power again.

And then I was out the door and racing down the street. If I could lose him, I could double back and get to the bus station. It didn't take long to disabuse me of that notion.

A couple blocks down, I was pretty sure I wasn't going to catch my bus because I could still hear him shrieking behind me, the scraping of his claws on the cement, and I didn't dare look back again to see how close he was. I had, early on in the chase, just in time to see him leap into the air as a man, his body twisting, and convulsing in a sickening way to come down as the dog.

The dog shape was a lot faster.

I just ran, breath coming in harsh pants as I wove down

the streets, deeper into the city, dodging people on the sidewalk who looked shocked as they tried to avoid a collision with me and then screamed when they saw what was chasing me.

Leaving had been a really, really stupid idea. I swore at myself. Of course I would choose the dumbest fucking course I could. All because for some God-awful petty reason I had to stick it to Greg. Look, I know what my motivation was, and it wasn't well-based in self-preservation. Glad to hear that you're smarter than I am. Does it make you feel good?

I dodged into the street itself, to the sound of squealing tires and honking horns, and then there was the solid CRUNCH as one of the cars couldn't stop in time. There was pained screaming and groaning, and I dared to take a peek behind me. The big black dog thing was on the ground, snarling and trying to get up, but part of it was stuck under the car that had hit it.

"Ha!" I laughed. "Take that, bitch!"

Except then, with a screech of crumpling metal, it pulled itself free.

"Oh, fuck." I turned to run again.

And ran straight into Greg. I yelped because it felt like I had run into a steel wall. He wrapped his arms around me so tightly I wasn't sure I could breathe, and he dragged me into the air.

∞

He took me back to his building. When he landed on the roof, he practically dropped me before grabbing me by the arm and hauling me toward the door.

"Ow!" I yelped, more out of surprise than because it hurt. "Ow! Stop it!" I tried to yank my arm away, but I might as well have been caught in a bear trap. His hold was like iron.

He turned to face me, but I was still stumbling forward, so I slammed into his chest again. I only stayed upright because he was holding onto me.

"What the fuck were you thinking, Meg?!" he shouted at me.

"You didn't tell me I was basically going to be a prisoner!" I spat at him, immediately on the defensive. Because I couldn't just admit to him that he was right.

"You—" he sputtered. He ran his free hand through his hair. "You couldn't just ask?!"

"Ask what?" I snarled, trying to yank my arm free again. "If I was allowed to leave?"

"You," he said again looming over me, too close for comfort when I was trapped, "have no idea what he is capable of. You couldn't just ask why all the caution?"

I hesitated. Because I hadn't really. I had just made snarky comments about it. I narrowed my eyes at him. "Would you have told me why?"

I saw the hesitation in his eyes. He was hiding something.

That hurt. Although I guess I hadn't really given him a reason to trust me, especially if I wasn't willing to trust him either.

I stepped back from him as far as I could with my arm still in his vice-like grip and repeated my question. "Would you have told me why?"

"I can't," he said, but it sounded like a plea.

"Can't or won't?"

"Can't."

Well, this was a wrinkle. I thought for a minute. "Can we go back to the field?" Could I push him toward ignoring whatever orders he was under?

"No."

"Okay," I said slowly, "so, what are we going to do?"

"We are going to go back down to my apartment. And you aren't going to steal any more key cards or attack any more people."

"It was technically only the two," I muttered. Wait, three? Was it three? Doesn't matter.

He huffed and echoed my thoughts. "The number of people isn't the important part."

"What about the thing back there? Don't you have to go make sure he's not murdering more people?"

"No. The others are on it. Observation only, get involved if he goes after anyone."

"They're letting him go?!"

"Meg," he said. "Do you know how he found you?"

"Don't change the subject," I snapped. "Why aren't they taking him down?" He was right there! In public! Couldn't they just overwhelm him with numbers? Surely, he couldn't turn that many powers back at once!

He hesitated again.

"Don't tell me, you can't say." I tried to yank my arm away again, and this time he let me go. "Tell your bosses I said they're assholes. And that maybe they should try for transparency." I stalked over to the door and waited for him. Because I wanted to know what their endgame was. And I don't appreciate being expected to cool my heels while they get around to whatever it is they're doing. Maybe what I should be doing is being nosy. How much could I get Greg to tell me? Because if I do anything well, it's badger people. If I could get enough info from him, maybe I could be more proactive.

He followed me and opened the door. I slipped through

ahead of him, stomping down the stairs to his floor and then glared at the wall until he reached me and opened that door, too. He waited for me to go through first. When we reached his apartment, I saw the front door on the floor of the hallway, crumpled and bowed. The wall across from where it used to hang was crumbling.

"Um . . ." I said, staring at it.

"You locked me in, and I didn't know if I had time to wait for them to get a new keycard coded to it," he said calmly. "They're replacing it later today. Until then, you get to sit right down on the couch where I can see you."

"The other doors are still up," I said, although the one door certainly explained why he didn't seem too worried about being contained. It made me less concerned about being trapped. If he was already that determined to protect me, stupid escape attempts aside, it might extend to protection from his bosses if they turned on him.

"Yeah, because Bolt brought me an extra card for the common doors. Otherwise, they would need to be replaced too." He gave me a gentle nudge through the doorway. "Go sit down."

I went in and flopped down onto the closest corner of the couch. He hung back by the wall, leaning against it, arms crossed. I watched him watching me.

"Is this seriously what we're going to do?"

"Yes," he said.

"You're going to stand there all day?"

"Yes."

"Could you just come sit down? You're making me twitchy staring at me like that."

He walked over to the couch and stared down at me. "Do you really want to be stuck sitting between me and the

72

corner?"

He had a point. I edged down the couch, making sure there would be generous spacing between us. He took the spot I had just vacated, resting one hand on the arm of the couch, the other slung across the back. His fingers brushed against my back.

"Sorry," he said, moving his hand away.

"So…" I said after a couple minutes of silence. "Are we going to just sit here and stare at the wall?" If he would talk to me, maybe I could get an ally. Okay, mission "Get on Greg's Good Side" in full swing. I don't "damsel in distress" well. I wanted a partner, not a watchdog. In not dying.

He leaned forward and grabbed one of the remotes, flipping through channels past the news, an action movie, and football before he settled on a cartoon. "This is about your maturity level, right?" he said.

I stuck my tongue out at him. He chuckled as he set the remote back down.

Setting my phone down on the coffee table, which thank God I had managed to hold onto it when I ran from the café, I realized I had left behind his bookbag and therefore the rest of my stuff, which included my new charger because I had just yanked the phone free when I took off.

"Um, so about the café—" I said, and I could literally feel his interest sharpen.

"Yeah?" he asked.

"I, um, kind of left your bookbag there."

"My bookbag," he said flatly.

"Yeah, well, I had borrowed it because I didn't want to be lugging my suitcase around—"

"Stole," he said. "You mean you stole my bookbag."

"Same difference."

He just watched me, eyes narrowed.

"Anyway, it's got some of my stuff and my phone charger was plugged in, and I kind of need it."

With a sigh he pulled out his phone and started texting. Being nosy, I peeked at it. He ignored me. Probably because it looked like there were no other messages sent to that number, so all I could read was "528 Whitehall Street, bookbag and charger. Watch yourself."

A message pinged back. "On it."

He tossed his phone onto the table. There was a cracking sound. "Damn it," he said, picking it up and examining it. "They're gonna start taking these out of my paycheck." This time he set it down very gently.

"Maybe they should get you a Nokia?"

He snorted. "I don't think they even make those anymore."

There was the rushing whoosh of wind, and Greg's bookbag hit my leg before it hit the floor.

"Delivery," said the woman who had appeared in his apartment. She didn't look how I would've expected someone with speed to look. She was built like she could give Greg a run for his money in terms of strength. But maybe I should be working on my "speedsters are wispy, frail-looking things" preconceptions. Obviously, she had to be a speedster. No one else could've gone and gotten my stuff that quickly. Are you questioning me? Maybe you need to work on your preconceptions too.

"Thanks," he grunted.

She looked at the TV. "Really, cartoons?"

"It's what was on," he shrugged.

"Yeah? Is it because you're stuck with the kid?" she said, gesturing at me.

"Wow, great insult," I said. I mean, come on, I'm twenty-seven. Not a kid.

She leaned over Greg, who yanked his head back out of the way, and addressed me directly. "Maybe next time don't be such a fuck up."

"Uh-huh. I'll be sure to take that advice into consideration when I, like, give a shit."

She moved back from the couch. "Some of us are going down to the taproom later tonight. You're invited," said the Speedster, who was now pointedly ignoring me. "She's not."

"Oooh," I said. "Is that supposed to hurt my feelings? Because you're gonna have to try a lot harder than that."

"Can't," he said.

"Why not?" she asked, sounding irritated.

"You know why not."

"They'll have your door back up by that time. Just lock her in."

Greg just looked at her.

She rolled her eyes. "When you decide to be a less serious person, you know where to find me."

"Yup," he said. And then she was gone.

"That Bolt?" I asked.

"Yup."

"Haven't met her before."

"That's because she refused to try and recruit you. Said she had better things to waste her time on."

"Huh. I think I kind of like her."

He gave me a side eye. "You would," he said.

I would've tried hitting him with one of the couch pillows, but I was worried it would explode, and he would probably expect me to clean up all the feathers. I might be petty, but I draw the line at creating more work for myself. So I settled for knocking the remotes off the coffee table when I put my feet up on it.

Yeah, I'm already failing at the "good side" part, aren't I?

He sighed and nudged me with the hand behind my back. "Are you going to pick those up?"

"Nope," I said.

He leaned forward and turned so he could look me in the eye. "Seriously?"

"Seriously."

"Are you always like this?"

"Like what?" I asked innocently. We stared at each other for a long beat. Finally, he sighed again and scooped the remotes off the floor. He set them down on the coffee table next to my feet. I smirked and started to shift to knock them off again. He caught my legs, his right hand against my calves, the fingers of his left hand still pressing against my back.

"I know what you're about to do, and don't you dare."

"Know me that well already?" I said, grinning at him.

He was fighting not to smile back. "I think I can safely say I'm at least getting to know you."

"Getting to know you, getting to know all about you—" I sang at him.

"What is that from?" he asked.

"*The King and I,*" I told him, and he looked confused. "The musical?"

"You watch musicals?" he asked.

"I watch a lot of different stuff," I said. What? I'm cultured.

"You just don't seem like you'd be into musicals." He had let go of my legs and leaned back into the arm of the couch so that he was still turned toward me.

"Why not?" I asked. I mean, who isn't into musicals?

People sing, they dance, everything is wrapped up with a happy ending by the third act.

"They just don't seem like something you'd be interested in," he said.

"That reasoning is lame," I told him, taking my feet off the table and pulling one leg up onto the couch so I could twist to face him. "What about me makes you think I wouldn't like musicals?"

He was silent, his brow furrowed.

"See?" I said. "You don't have a reason. You just assumed I wouldn't be into them."

"Why are you into them?"

"Because they're fun."

"They're fun?"

"Yes," I said. "You got Netflix on this thing?"

"No. I don't watch a lot of TV, so a subscription service seemed kind of pointless."

I gaped at him. "How do you not have Netflix? Everyone has Netflix."

He waved at the TV. "So, sign into your account. It has the app; I just don't have an account."

Well now I was stuck because I didn't have an account either.

He smirked at me. "You don't have one either do you?"

Fine, time to switch tactics. "This thing have YouTube?"

"Yes."

I waved a hand at it. "So, go to YouTube."

"Why?"

"I'm going to look up *Hairspray*, and you're going to watch it."

He didn't move, he just watched me. "*Hairspray?*"

"Yes! The new one with John Travolta and Queen Latifah. It's amazing, you'll love it. I mean, if it's still up on YouTube. If not, you can watch the original, it's still good." When he still didn't move, I reached for the remotes myself. "Fine, show me how your TV works, and I'll look it up."

He was faster than I was, his arm snaking out to grab the remotes before I could and holding them just out of reach.

"Hey!" I snatched at them, and he moved his arm further up, away from me. I paused, considering him through narrowed eyes. "Give me the remotes."

"Or you'll what?" he asked grinning at me.

I lunged at him, practically scrambling up him to get the remotes from his hand. He leaned back over the arm of the couch, pulling them out of my reach again. And then, the whole thing tilted over. The couch crashed onto its side; Greg hit the floor with his back. Something cracked, and I heard the remotes clatter as he dropped them to brace against the floor, his legs keeping the couch in place. His other arm was wrapped around me because I had landed on his chest, my legs uncomfortably twisted against his and the seat of the couch.

"Are you alright?" he asked.

"Fine," I said, trying to push off him. He moved his arm. I rolled to the side and got up. "That's what you get for flirting with me."

I know I was complicit in the flirting, shut up. He's the one who tipped the couch over.

His lips twitched, and he had that amused look in his eyes again. "Was I?" he asked.

I glared at him, "You know you were, quit it." There was a flash of disappointment across his face. It bothered me that I put it there, and I flicked my eyes away, fixing them on the bookbag.

"You still going to make me watch musicals?" he asked from the floor.

"Oh no, I don't think you deserve to get to know the wonder that is *Hairspray* anymore." I snagged the bookbag up, swinging it up onto my back before I flounced off to the bathroom, leaving him and the couch stuck to the floor. Well, stuck until he figured out how to get up without the couch tilting over onto anything else.

∞

Since I had my stuff back, I took the opportunity to take a shower. A very long one, because he had this HUGE walk-in shower with freaking showerheads everywhere. Like, who wouldn't take advantage of standing in a monsoon of hot water? Also, this is what your tax dollars are paying for. Just think you should take note of that.

I was dressed in a tank and a fresh pair of jeans and was trying to tame my hair back into a ponytail when he knocked on the door.

"Are you coming back out at any point?"

I opened the door. "You know, I thought I might just live in here."

He actually cracked a grin, until he saw the bruise that was wrapped around my upper arm. He seemed to fold in on himself, his eyes focused on the floor, as he took a half-step back from me.

"I hurt you," he sounded distressed.

I looked down at my arm, then back at him. "It's just a bruise." Besides, I was pretty sure I had done most of the damage trying to yank myself free. His grip might have been impossible to get out of, but it hadn't been tight enough to cause the marks if I hadn't been resisting.

"That is entirely beside the point. I hurt you," his eyes were shadowed. "I'm sorry," he said quietly.

"I think I can forgive you," I said, trying to slip past him. For once he moved out of my way without any sort of protest. That put me on alert. "What is your problem?"

He looked surprised. "Problem?"

"Yes, problem. You look like you kicked a puppy. It was an accident, it's just a bruise, I'll live. Stop moping."

He stared at me, flabbergasted. Ha, that was much better than the guilty, hangdog expression that was on his face. Wait, why wasn't I reveling in him feeling guilty in the first place?

Oh my God. I was actually starting to kind of like him and his stupid do-gooderness. Damn it.

"Shoo," I said to him. "Go do something other than stare at me."

He didn't move.

I flopped back down on the couch; he must have set it right while I was in the bathroom. They also must've finally fixed his door, because it was firmly back in place. I crossed my arms, propped my feet up on his coffee table and glared at him. My stomach rumbled.

He took that as a lifeline. "When did you last eat?"

I shrugged. Not since the night before, when I ate the last of his boiled eggs. But I wasn't telling him that. It's not like I had time to while I was on the run. And then I had gotten distracted. Look, some of us get involved in what we're doing and forget to eat at times. No, I was not distracted by Dudley Do-Right and his muscles!

He sighed. I could see he was caught between the need to do something and follow his orders to not leave me alone. I decided to take pity on him.

"You have any eggs left?"

"No," he scrubbed at his face.

"The croissant sandwich thing was pretty good," I offered up.

He hesitated.

"I won't move from this exact spot on the couch," I said.

He narrowed his eyes.

"Scout's honor," I told him. "Besides," I said as I turned my attention back to the TV. "You have the keycard. Where would I even go?"

That seemed to reassure him, and he headed out the door. "If I find you anywhere else in this apartment, I will tie you to the couch."

"I dare you to try."

He chuckled.

CHAPTER SIX

A while after he brought back food, Greg got tired of cartoons. Which, if he hadn't knocked the couch over, we could've been watching musicals. Just saying. He got up and started pulling cleaning supplies out from under the kitchen sink. I scooted back over into the corner of the couch so I could lean on the arm and watch him.

"What're you doing?" I asked him.

"Cleaning," he said.

"Why?"

He gave me a look. "Have you seen a maid service in here?"

I rolled my eyes. "No, not why are you cleaning, why are you doing it now?"

He was wiping down the kitchen counters with soapy water. "Because if I'm stuck here, as pleasant as the company is, I might as well do something productive."

"That's a first."

"What is?" he asked, which wasn't what I expected to hear. I would've immediately focused on the "do something productive statement" and stepped right into the "I'm plenty productive" argument.

I floundered for a second before focusing on the first part. "No one's called my company pleasant before."

"Hmm," he said, apparently choosing the diplomatic path. He had started on wiping down the cabinets too. Then he paused, rummaged under the sink again and set more rags on the counter. He filled another small bowl with soapy water. "If you want to help, the tables need to be wiped down, too."

I set my chin in my hand, elbow resting on the arm of the couch. "I don't know, I'm pretty comfortable here."

He snorted, lips twitching, and set the supplies he was using down on the counter by the sink. From another cabinet he pulled out a broom and dustpan, which he set down next to the couch. "You sure?" he asked me.

"Yup," I said.

He lifted the couch up. The whole thing up in the air like it weighed no more than a feather to him. He tilted it just enough that I was cradled against the back of it. I yanked my legs up onto it with me and grabbed at the arm with both hands. I felt it shift as he changed his grip and grabbed the broom where it was leaning against the coffee table.

"Still comfortable?" he asked.

"Yup," I said, although now I was crouched on the couch, my feet sunk in the corner created by the seat and back.

"You know I can hold you up here all day, right?"

"So, you're going to hold both me and the couch hostage until I agree to help you clean?" The couch bounced a bit. I tightened my grip on the arm.

"Pretty much," he said, and I could hear the amusement in his voice.

I took a peek over the edge of the back. The drop wasn't that far. I shifted my weight, dangling my legs over it.

"You have fun with that," I said.

The couch shifted again, tumbling me down so I was lying with my back against the seat cushions. Greg had set it on the floor. He leaned over the back of it, arms crossed, grinning down at me. "Resistance is futile," he quoted.

I snorted. "Are you flirting with me again?"

"Absolutely."

I had to flounder again, because I wasn't sure how, or even if I wanted to, respond to that.

He took pity on my sudden inability to speak and held out a hand to me. "Come on, I'll help you up." I eyed his hand for a moment, trying to decide which direction I wanted to head in. No romances. Right? Fuck. He waited, unwavering. Slowly, I reached out and put my hand in his. His fingers tightened gently around mine, and he reached down with his free arm to scoop me up by my shoulders and set me on the floor behind the couch. He was still holding my hand when he snagged the broom from where he had set it against the couch when he put it down. "So, tables or floors?" he asked me.

"Tables," I said, because I needed my hand back before I did something stupid. What? I've already told you a girl has needs, and he has a really nice smile when he's not trying to boss me around. He released my hand, setting the broom against the island as he passed by it. He came back bearing the second bowl and a couple rags.

"Here," he said. I took them, and then headed for the dining room table. I considered playing dumb, but he had seen the condition of my apartment before he threw the door into the fridge. I don't go many places when I'm not being stalked by a murderous man-dog, so I tend to keep the apartment clean anyway.

But he had gone back to being silent, and it was making

my back itch again. "So," I said, "how long have you been in the hero business?"

"A decade, give or take," he said, wiping down the appliances now.

"So, since-?"

"Straight out of college."

"Which one?" He looked like someone who would've gone to a Big 10, probably on a football scholarship. Would they have allowed him to play sports? Or would that fall under the unfair advantages rule? There's a reason heroes don't go into professional sports. There aren't any hard-written rules about it, but good luck getting a contract if you're a known quantity.

"Private," he said. "You won't have heard of it. I got recruited for hero work right out of high school, so they set me up with a scholarship." He was dumping the dirty water into the sink, rinsing the bowl and filling it with clean.

Well, I was right about the scholarship part. We were silent again, my rag making slow circles on the table.

"You have to get more water on it every so often," he said over my head, sounding amused.

"I know that," I said, following the words with the action. He leaned against the table, so now he was in my way. I looked up at him. "I'm trying to clean here."

"You already did that section. You'll wear a hole in it."

I huffed. "Maybe I just think it needs to be waxed on and waxed off."

He grinned at me again, and I noticed how warm his eyes were. I looked back down at the table. "You go to college?" he asked me.

"You read my file. I'm sure the answer for everything about me is in there right down to my favorite color." I moved away from him. I had not gone to college; technically I counted as a high school drop-out. I basically disappeared from my hometown right after the disaster of a high school party because my parents had moved us out of state, and I had never enrolled anywhere else or tried for a GED. I mean, if not for that night, I might have managed a track scholarship for college. I might not be anywhere close to Bolt, but I was fast enough. But I didn't. How could I have gone back to my life like it never happened? New town, yeah, but I didn't deserve a new life. I even gave up running entirely, and I used to love it.

Oh, you're surprised I ran track? That I did normal shit? Well, here's a shocker for you: I wanted to be normal. How many teenagers want to be weird? To not fit in? Before the party, I had basically refused to use the whispers for years once I had conscious control over them. Maybe if I hadn't, the results of that night wouldn't have been so extreme.

"I stuck to the skills section," he said. "So, what is your favorite color?"

I smirked at him. "Wouldn't you like to know?" But I was grateful for the subject change; it pulled me away from my own thoughts.

"You can't leave a wet rag just sitting on the wood. It'll warp," he said, gently pulling the rag from me and taking over the wipe-down of the table. The feel of his fingers on mine lingered. I wiped my hands off on my jeans. Didn't help, because now I had wet marks on my legs, and I could still feel his hand on mine.

But I had managed to get him to take back over the cleaning again. He finished wiping down the dining table and it's matching chairs and moved over to the coffee table. He tossed the remotes onto the couch, wiped it down, and then moved them back. Back over to the sink to pour out the water.

And then he was wiping everything back down with the clean water. I stayed by the dining table, uncertain and off balance. He made his way back around to me.

He was in my space again. "Meg," he started. He was too close to me, so I stepped past him, across to the kitchen, and grabbed the broom.

"Floors," I said, and headed across the apartment to the bedroom side to put as much space between us as possible. I wanted the complication that getting involved with him would bring, and that scared me.

The irony of the side of the apartment I went to is not lost on me.

∞

There were screams all around me. Bodies writhing and clawing at each other and themselves. The carpet was sticky and matted with blood. As I stumbled toward the door, they desperately tried to fling themselves away from me. Someone bumped into me, knocking me off balance, skin hanging in shreds from his body. He reared back as I staggered, and he flung himself into the group of bodies rather than stay by me and the whispers. A hand plucked at my ankles, and I kicked it away before I looked down.

It had no face. And a gaping hole where the mouth should have been.

"Meeeeeggggg," it called.

∞

I sat up. I was left blinking in the dark, staring in the direction of the windows.

Something was outside.

"Meeeeeeggggg," it called, the sound slightly muffled.

A hand clamped over my mouth, an arm wrapped itself around my waist and pulled me back toward the body it was attached to. "Mphhf!" I bucked.

"Meg," Greg's voice hissed in my ear. "Stop."

I sagged back against him.

"I'm going to move my hand. Don't scream."

"Mphhf!"

The hand let go.

I twisted to face him as best I could. "Why the fuck would you do that in the first place!" I hissed at him.

"Screaming really hurts my ears, and I wasn't sure how you were going to react to him."

"In case you can't tell," I continued to hiss out the words, "I'm not some wilting flower who screams over every jump scare."

"Noted," he said. "Don't move, don't acknowledge him."

There was a sound like nails scraping along a chalkboard. A shiver went up my spine.

"How does he keep finding me?" My voice sounded strangled.

"I don't know," he said grimly.

His arm was still wrapped around my waist, and I tugged at it. I wanted to be behind him, so he would be between me and the thing.

Look, sometimes a little fear is a healthy thing. Putting the ridiculously strong man between me and the murdering demon creature was a better idea than staying exposed. Especially when said murdering demon creature wanted to specifically murder me.

There was a muffled bang as it tried hitting the window.

I squeaked and tried to climb over Greg to get behind him.

He looked down at me, slightly amused. "He's not getting in here. We're just going to wait until he gives up for the night." But he let go of me and moved to place himself between the windows and me.

"What if he doesn't give up? We're just gonna sit here all night?"

"Yup."

"What if he still doesn't go away after that?"

"Then we'll reassess the situation."

I did not like this plan. I also wasn't used to feeling this useless. The whispers were at my back, and they felt . . . reluctant?

"Meg." Now it was Greg's turn to sound strangled. "You can't draw on the fear right now."

I hadn't even noticed I was doing it. "Sorry," I muttered, letting it go.

There was another bang at the windows.

"I know you're in there, Meg. Come out, come out and play." The red eyes were at the window, pressed against whatever not-glass material it was made of. "You can't hide from me. You have to come outside eventually."

Fuck no I didn't. I had a building full of heroes between the exit and me, and this time I wanted it to stay that way. I just had to catch the interest of something that not only wanted me dead but could float sixty stories in the air. Or did it actually have wings? I mean, it shifted from a man to a dog thing, why not wings? I didn't really want to get closer to the windows to find out the answer to my question, so I stayed huddled against Greg's back while it hovered outside, waiting.

When I woke up, Greg had moved me over and tucked me back in. He was still next to me, sitting against the back of the couch, legs stretched out along the mattress, arms crossed, chin resting on his chest. I sat up and looked out the windows. Nothing there, just sunlight streaming in.

"He left a while ago," Greg said.

"I thought you were asleep."

"I was," he said, eyes still closed. "I'm going back to sleep."

A phone pinged down in the living room.

With a groan, he got up and headed down the stairs. I watched him while he picked up the phone and read whatever message had come in. He grumbled as he set it back down, grabbed some clean clothes and headed to the bathroom.

"What is it?" I called over the railing.

"They called a meeting. I'll bring breakfast when I get back." He closed the bathroom door behind him. I heard the shower start.

Because I had nothing better to do, I checked my phone.

Seven missed calls and a voicemail from work where they told me I was fired for being a no-show.

What the fuck.

I wanted to throw the phone, but if I didn't have the money to replace it while I was employed, I definitely didn't have the money to replace it now.

It was a terrible job anyway.

I was still sniffling and fighting back angry tears when Greg came out of the bathroom. He didn't bother with the stairs; he came right over the railing, landing on the bed next to me.

Guess it was a good thing his apartment had such a high

ceiling.

"What happened?" he demanded. "Are you alright? Did he come back?" He was looking around, out the windows, worried he had missed something.

"I got fired," I said, embarrassed by the tears. I was trying to hide my face and wipe them away at the same time.

"Oh," he continued looking around. "I don't, uh, I don't have any tissues."

Apparently, that meant he was going to settle for whipping off his shirt and handing it to me.

"Who are you?" I started giggling. "William Shatner?"

He looked confused, and that set me off further. It was this very odd mixture of laughing and crying.

"Are you - are you having hysterics again?" he asked cautiously.

The giggling had stopped, and I was using his shirt to wipe off the tears. "You honestly can't tell me you don't know about William Shatner and his constant shirt removal. I've never even watched *Star Trek,* and I know about it."

"Oh," he said. "I guess it just never really came up before. You want me to go have a word with your manager?"

"God no. It was a lousy job anyway."

If I said it enough, maybe I would believe I didn't need that shitty job.

"Uh huh," he said, like he didn't entirely believe me. "I have to go. Will you be okay?"

"Yup. I have a shirt," I said, giving him a smile.

There was a pause where we gazed at each other, a beat where I could have moved away, and then his lips were on mine, soft and hesitant. I couldn't think. I just responded and I flung my arms around his neck. He pulled me into him, his hands on my back, in my hair, and I shivered. Our lips pressed together, my heart pounding. I was breathless.

Oh fuck.

I yanked my head back, full on deer-in-headlights in that instant. I was trying to catch my breath, and he was staring back at me. We might have been mirror images in that moment. Our arms were still wrapped around each other. I desperately wanted both to go back to the minute before and to stay in the spell of it at the same time. My heart was racing; there was no way he could miss the way it was thudding.

"Meg," he said, and in response my heart fluttered.

Oh fuck. Jesus, I would fall for a hero, a knight in, well, not shining armor, I mean, his body is the armor, I mean, I'm just digging the hole deeper. Stop laughing at me!

I needed out of his arms before this went further. Slowly I pulled my arms off his neck and cleared my throat, looking down, away, anywhere but his face. "You said you had to go?"

"Yes," he said. "Go. I have to go." He sounded dazed and as breathless as I felt.

"You said that already," I told him, looking back up at his face.

He blinked; his eyes focused again. "Meeting, right. I'll be back. Will you wait for me?"

"I can't really go anywhere, remember?" I said, half teasing.

That seemed to startle him fully back down to earth. He gave me a sheepish grin, let go of me and headed down the stairs. He grabbed another shirt before he went out the door. And I was locked in.

I wasn't totally mad about it this time.

∞

He didn't have breakfast with him when he came back. He came through the door, slamming it behind him. I could feel the impact vibrate through the floor and the living room couch where I was sitting; the stools shuddered and bounced a bit under the kitchen island. I stared at him as he strode across the floor and then flipped the dining room table into the wall. It exploded, splinters and debris bouncing off the wall and back off him. There was wood dust in the air.

"Bad meeting?" I asked weakly, having backed up into the corner of the couch farthest from him. Oh my God, Meg, shut up! Not the time to be a smart ass.

"Yes," he snarled, still facing the remains of the table. "Those fucking idiots."

He started pacing the space between the table remnants and where his bed stood, which meant he was constantly passing by the couch I was on. He stopped, facing me. Right now, the length of the couch didn't feel like enough space.

"What do you absolutely need to take with you?" he demanded.

"What? Why?"

He was still snarling, "He left another message, and now they want me to use you as bait. To draw him out. Because they can't fucking find him, but he can sure as shit find you!"

"Apparently," he ranted as he paced, "they find that level of risk to you *acceptable*. Because it's perfectly *acceptable* to set someone down in front of that fucking thing when you're not the one at risk!" He slammed a fist down onto the kitchen island. I heard it crack, the stone shifting, and the floor shuddered again.

Okay, so the level of rage was sort of understandable in

the circumstances, but he was scaring me. I was pressed back as far into the couch as I could get, my heart hammering in my chest. I was afraid of attracting his attention. Just because I could take him down if I had to didn't mean I wanted to.

I forgot he could hear my heart.

He looked over at me. "Meg," he said, his voice hoarse now. "Meg, I'm sorry. I don't—" he took a shuddering breath. "They don't understand what he'll do to you if a trap doesn't work. I know. I know what he does; I've seen the results. I can't risk you that way."

"Can't or won't?" I asked.

"Both," he said.

Cautiously, I unfolded a bit. When he stayed back by the counter, I unfolded the rest of the way, setting my feet on the floor.

"Okay," I said. "So, what are we going to do?"

"What of your stuff do you absolutely have to have with you? Are you carrying anything irreplaceable?"

"I can't really afford to replace any of it."

He made a frustrated noise. "No, I mean, emotional value. Literally can't be replaced even if you have the cash to do it with."

"No." Which wasn't quite true, my stuff had emotional value to me because I didn't have the cash to replace it. But I knew what he meant, and it didn't seem like the best time to argue the semantics of it. But I had a question of my own. "What was the message?"

Greg hesitated.

"What was the message?" I repeated, irritation sharpening my tone. After a moment he pulled out his phone, tapped and scrolled, came over to the couch and held his phone out to me.

"If anyone asks, I didn't show you this." I took the phone and looked down at the screen. It was a photo of the side of a building, nondescript concrete. It could have been anywhere in the city. But I knew: it was this building. A body lay at the bottom of the wall; it looked like one of the security guards from the night I ran. "He had a family," Greg said. "Red Eye took him out when he left at the end of his shift."

The message was written on the concrete in blood. "I can taste your dreams," it read.

"That's not creepy at all," I said, handing the phone back to Greg. He didn't comment on the fact that my hand was shaking. And with his fingers brushing mine there was no way he had missed it. He slipped the phone back into his pocket.

"Okay, you saw the message. You need to come with me. We're leaving."

"And going where?"

"I'm taking you to a safe house."

"I thought this was a safe house."

"Meg." Again, the frustrated tone. "I need you to trust me. We need to leave, and it needs to be now." He held out his hand. "Please."

Slowly I put my hand in his and he pulled me to my feet, and then into his chest. He wrapped his arms around me and then buried his face against the top of my head, nose in my hair. He didn't move.

"Um, Greg?" Because as nice as it was to feel safe and protected in that moment, he had just said we needed to hurry. I tried to squirm back because I also hadn't had any one person touch me this often since I was sixteen, so despite my blossoming, okay blossomed, feelings for him, I needed some space. He didn't let go. If anything, his grip tightened. "Greg?" I said again.

"I'm going to need you to fight me," he said. "And try not to scream right in my ear."

"Wha—"

He slung me over his shoulder like I was a sack of potatoes.

"What the Hell?!" I shrieked. I tried to kick at him, but he had me by my legs, and I couldn't get any leverage. I hit him in the back, but that just hurt my hands. Then he had us out in the hall and was hauling me along at a fast clip. I shrieked again and tried to fling myself off his shoulder, but he had already grabbed my hips with his free hand, so I was stuck, bouncing against him. I didn't dare fight back with the whispers because that would leave me trapped with the other heroes and the politicians who wanted me used as bait. And even if I took all of them down, that left me with no help against Red Eye.

So instead, I screamed and swore at him.

He was in the stairwell and headed for the roof.

"Put me down! Please, please just put me down," I resorted to pleading.

He had the door to the roof open and was shouldering it out of the way, and then he slid me off his shoulder so that his free arm was wrapped around my back, my side snug against his chest, and he leapt into the air.

CHAPTER SEVEN

He took us out into the country, landing in a field outside a small town.

"I'm going to put you down," he said. "Don't run. And don't do your thing."

He set me down, and I scrambled away from him. Once I had a few feet of space, I turned to glare at him. He was a half-step toward me, poised, and I suspected if I hadn't stopped when I did, he would have chased after me.

"Explain to me why I shouldn't do my thing." The whispers were at my back, and they were eager.

"I am buying us some time before they realize I absconded with you rather than following their stupid-ass plan."

"So you kidnap me?" I asked, incensed.

"I was told to inform you that your cooperation was required to bait their trap. Would you have cooperated?"

I opened my mouth, shut it, thought for a moment. "No," I said.

"Would you have fought me?"

I glared at him, irritated that he could read me that well. "Yes."

"There you go," he said. "A believable exit. They've got it on camera, and won't know I just did a runner until we don't show up on site."

I stood there, considering, wavering between anger and relief. Anger that he didn't feel it necessary to share the plan with me before he broke us out. Relief that I at least wasn't currently in some government official's game of chance.

"You could've made that a little clearer at the start," I finally said.

"If I thought you wouldn't have wasted time arguing with me, I would've."

Fair point.

We were both silent, warily watching each other. He spoke first.

"We need to go into town; we're going to need ground transport."

"Why?" I asked. I resisted, apprehensive that I had only switched which chess master was presiding over me. I didn't want anyone, Greg included, making decisions for me.

"Because where we're going has anti-aircraft guns, and he will try to shoot me down."

"Excuse me?"

"Vigilante," he repeated slowly, "has anti-aircraft guns, and he will try to shoot me down if I come flying in."

"I thought you said he was freelance?"

"He is. That doesn't mean some of his benefactors aren't wealthy. And some of them like being able to call a hero directly just because they heard a creak in the attic."

"That is just - that's ridiculous."

There was another moment of silence.

"Are we good?" he asked me.

"I'm not ready to answer that question yet."

He just nodded. "Okay. We still need to go into town. Are you coming with me?"

"Do I have a choice?"

"Meg, I will follow you wherever you want to go. But please, let me protect you the best way I know how."

"What if I don't want you protecting me?" I snapped. I regretted it immediately.

He looked absolutely crushed in that moment. His face fell; eyes downcast, his whole body seemed to draw in on itself. The words were already out, and I couldn't take them back. He cleared his throat. "I will respect whatever decision you make. But he will find you, and he will kill you, and it won't be a gentle death, Meg. Please, don't bring that down on yourself because you don't want me."

I couldn't look him in the eye. "Okay," was all I said.

"Okay?" he said, and I could hear the relief in his voice that I wasn't willing to die just to spite him. Would he hear the remorse that was in mine?

"Okay," I said, and I followed him into town.

∞

Once in town, he headed straight to a parking lot located behind a building and began testing the car doors.

"What are you doing?" I hissed following him.

"Do you see any buses out here?" he asked me.

"No, but you can't just—"

"Ha," he cut me off because the door to a sedan opened. "Get in, I need to hot wire it."

"You're stealing a car!?"

He looked at me. "Meg, get in the goddamn car."

I muttered under my breath, but I hauled myself over the

99

driver's seat and center console into the passenger seat. He sat
down and shut the door and then hit the locks. Then he was
pulling pieces off here and gently yanking out wires there, and I
had no idea what he was doing. The engine caught.

"Buckle up," he said, shifting into drive and hitting the
gas, and then he drove sedately out of the lot and up the main
street of town. It was a tiny, one-stop-light kind of a place, the
street made up of little one-story buildings, some with facades
to make them appear taller. A bank, hardware store,
secondhand clothing, hair salon and attorney of law crowded
together in a row off my side of the car.

I just stared at him. "Seriously?"

"You want the cops looking our way? Driving it like you
stole it will definitely get their attention."

"You don't think someone will notice their car going
down the street without them?"

"Most people aren't that observant."

"You know this from experience?"

"No comment," he said.

"You were a nightmare as a teenager, weren't you?"

"Let's just say I might have had to learn a couple hard
lessons."

I was silent, because I hadn't exactly become a paragon
of society after my own hard lesson.

He must have sensed something was up. "Hey, not
everyone deals with trauma in the same way. And your power,
it's a rough one to have to grow up with."

"Is that why you're all so convinced I'm going to
become a villain?" I asked, setting my feet up on the dash.

He tapped my leg. "Put your feet down."

"Why? Because I'll get our stolen car dirty?"

"No, because if we get in a wreck, your knees will end up

in your face, and the airbag will shatter your shins. So put your feet down."

I hastily set them back on the floor.

"I would hope your reaction time to avoid a wreck would be better than the average Joe's," I said because I couldn't help but needle him.

"Powers don't mean I don't make mistakes."

We were on winding country roads now, and he sped up. I stared out the windows, watching the scenery pass by. Trees, fields, fencing, cows, even a red barn. The silence quickly became unbearable, made all the worse by the tension between us.

"So," I said, "how far out does Vigilante live?"

"Far enough that he convinced someone to give him a helicopter."

"No wonder people think we should eat the rich," I muttered.

"You might as well just use full volume when you make those comments; I'm going to be able to hear them anyway."

We crested a hill, and a squat building appeared in the distance, quickly disappearing from view as we dipped back down below the thickening canopy of trees. "Almost there," Greg said, his shoulders tense as he swiveled in the seat, checking the area around us as he pushed the gas down further. The engine whined as the car sped up even more.

"Is there a reason you've decided this is the Indy 500?"

"I want to get inside before Red Eye realizes you're not in my apartment anymore." I didn't know how Greg would spot anything lurking in the woods we were barreling through. But his agitation was making me nervous.

He slowed the car as we approached a looming metal gate and fence topped by barbed wire. There was a callbox.

Greg stopped the car and rolled down the window; then he reached out and hit the button on the box. It buzzed. There was a long moment of crackling silence.

"What do you want?" came the voice on the other end.

"It's me. The politicians finally pissed me off. Let me in, I need your help."

There was another moment where the only sound was the crackle of static. Then the gate squealed as it began rolling out of the way. Greg revved the engine and sped up the long, gravel driveway. Past the unkempt yard and overgrown bushes, headed for the stairs leading up to a hulking square building, dark gray in color, that looked like it was made of stone. As far as I could tell, it had no windows. The whole thing had an air of having been abandoned.

There was a man waiting for us at the door into the building. The car slid to a stop, and Greg barely had it in park before he had shoved the door out of his way. It bounced into the yard. "Damn it," he said, but he didn't hesitate to do the same thing to my door when he reached the passenger side. "Out," he said. I started to open my mouth. "Don't fucking argue, Meg, just get out and go."

I clamped my mouth shut and climbed out of the car, and he hustled me up to the door, one hand on the small of my back.

"Gregor," said the man at the door.

"Virgil," Greg grunted. And then we were inside, and the man had shut the door behind us and was spinning a lock closed. Like the kind you would see in those old timey bank safes.

"Gregor?" I asked.

"Gregor the Fortress," said Vigilante, apparently also known as Virgil. He slapped Greg on the back, hard, then winced and shook his hand. "I always forget it's like smacking a concrete wall."

"Gregor, the Fortress?" And I couldn't hide the amusement in my voice. Because Greg hadn't told me his hero name. To be honest, it fit him. But the way Virgil was using it combined with what had to be his full given name definitely elevated it to the most ridiculous pseudonym I'd heard a hero use.

"Laugh it up. I didn't pick either name," Greg said.

We were following Virgil deeper in, across an empty expanse of floor to an interior wall, where he hauled another metal door open. There was a set of stairs leading down into darkness. Then there was a hum, and dull green lights along the treads lit up.

"Sometimes the generator takes a minute to kick on," he said.

Greg grunted and headed down the stairs. I hesitated at the top. He sighed and reached back for my hand. "Meg."

I pulled my hand away. And saw the hurt in his eyes. I stepped forward, slipping past him to continue down the stairs, and he followed me. Behind us, I could hear Virgil close the door, and again, the spinning of a lock.

The room at the bottom looked like a relatively normal living room. Other than the fact that the ceiling was low and concrete and that there were no windows. But there were couches, tables, bookcases, even a TV.

Virgil steered around us because I had paused only a few steps into the room, and Greg had stayed next to me. "You two know you can sit down, right? The couches aren't museum pieces. Although they're certainly old enough to qualify." He demonstrated by flinging himself into a chair and pulled a leg up, resting the ankle on the opposite knee. He indicated the rest of the seating. "Sit. We'll talk about whatever brought you here." Now that I had a chance to take a good look at him, I saw he was thin-faced, with a narrow nose, lanky, whipcord build with dark hair and a well-groomed beard.

Greg walked over and sat down on one of the couches facing Virgil. I hesitated back by the stairs. Both men watched me.

"We don't bite," Virgil said. I didn't respond. "Well," he said after a moment of silence, "who's your friend, Gregor?"

Greg winced. "Can you not call me that?"

"Who's your friend, Fortress?" Virgil said.

I snorted. Greg shot me a look. I cleared my throat and found the floor very interesting for a minute. Greg sighed.

"This is Meg."

"*The* Meg?"

"Yes, *the* Meg." Greg sounded mildly irritated.

"A pleasure, Meg," Virgil said in my direction. "Fascinating. She's shorter than I would have expected. But then, great things, small packages. All that fluff."

Vigilante was not how I expected either. He reminded me of Nicholas Cage. Right down to his mannerisms and the way he moved, the pitch and timbre of his voice. I wanted to ask if the resemblance was intentional.

I don't know, I expected someone who took everything way too seriously, and would always talk in a deep scary voice to sound intimidating. Virgil seemed to be a chameleon, flowing from affable to antagonistic all while appearing unruffled and cool. Somehow genial and uncordial in the same breath. His inconsistency was throwing me off balance, and I was already unsteady from the field, the ground uneven beneath me.

I chose to concentrate on a different subject. "*The* Meg?" I asked.

"Yes, you're famous, or is it infamous? I forget if they mean the same thing." Virgil waved at the couches again. "Sit. There's nowhere to run to from here; you might as well relax."

I took the seat furthest from both of them. Greg looked away from me.

"So," Virgil clapped his hands together, gamely ignoring the tension in the room. "What brings you here?"

Greg leaned forward. "He's after her."

Virgil straightened up. "Oh, is he now?"

"I'm sorry, but how much of his fucking history are you hiding from me?" I demanded. Because I might do some stupid, only kinda-sorta planned out things, but I would have to be a different class of idiot altogether not to come to the realization that Red Eye had been a problem for much longer than I had been aware of.

They both looked at me.

Virgil looked back at Greg. "You haven't told her?"

It sounded like Greg was grinding his teeth again. I wanted to snap at him not to do that before he wore them down to nubs.

"Well, I'm not going to wait around for you to get over whatever your feelings on this are," Virgil said. He turned toward me. "He likes to go after other villains. Kind of like you. It's why they haven't done anything about him before this."

I was unsure as to whether Virgil was calling me a villain or claiming I hunted them down. But either way, I was already angry and defensive.

"I do NOT go after anyone," I snapped at him. "They come after me first. Unlike some of you, I don't go hunting for the bad guys."

"Yeah, what was the thing with - what's his name -

Mirage?"

"He broke into my apartment! He—" I stopped because I didn't want to get into what he tried to do. Or the fact that I had lost my security deposit on that one too. The blood had soaked down into the subfloor and even into the studs in the walls. They told me it would've been cheaper for them if I had burnt the building down. The only reason they hadn't gone after me for the damage in court was I had frightened the shit out of the landlord. Not enough to keep him from keeping what he did have of my money though.

Virgil had steepled his fingers and was watching me with interest. "I like this one. You like her, Gregor?"

Greg was glaring at him, and I looked away.

"So," said Virgil. He seemed to really like that word. "Who was the last one he took out, Gregor?" When Greg didn't answer him, Virgil continued on. "What was her name - Patrice?"

"You know exactly what her name was," Greg said through gritted teeth. "You were there when she left."

"What was her power again? Shape shifting, wasn't it?" Virgil didn't stop. "She must have been a fun one before she turned. You have terrible taste in women my friend. Well, I do too." He shrugged. Then leaned forward like a new thought had occurred to him. "You still stuck with that table?"

I wasn't entirely sure if I was insulted or not. I did know I didn't like Virgil's attitude right now, even if he was giving me information Greg had been sitting on. "Shut up," I said, the figures curling around me.

"Or what? You'll attack me, Meg?" Virgil asked me.

"You don't want to test me," I said, the shadows stretching out along the floor from where my feet were resting, the whispers in my ears.

"Meg," Greg sounded tired. "Don't." I looked at him. "Don't," he repeated. I let the power go. It faded away with a sigh.

"I really do like her," Virgil said.

∞

Eventually Virgil had to feed us. He had spent the time it took to lead us to the kitchen needling Greg some more, this time about his sort-of meat free diet.

Eventually, he settled on making eggplant pizzas. "Julia Child's own recipe," he told me. Greg just grunted.

We watched him, sitting on stools in his kitchen. Heroes seemed to really like their big island countertops. I nudged Greg with my foot. "Look, someone who cooks."

He glared at me. I bristled. "Fine, I won't talk to you."

"You really shouldn't bother talking to him when he's in this kind of mood," Virgil said, setting plates of food in front of us. "For someone so indestructible, he's incredibly delicate, emotionally speaking."

Greg switched who he was glaring at. "I am not delicate."

"You're like a flower," Virgil said.

"A thorny one," I muttered.

Virgil chuckled and wagged a finger at me. "On the nose."

I glared at him. "Don't tell me you have super hearing, too."

"Oh, no, nothing like that. You're just much louder than you think you are."

I pushed back from the counter and got up. Virgil didn't look up from his plate. "Don't go poking around into too many things. Sometimes the stuff in the lab likes to blow up for no reason."

I wasn't sure if he was serious or not, but just in case, I avoided the door clearly marked Laboratory. Wandering around, I found his security room. As far as I could tell, he had a bird's eye view of every corner of his property. I left the room and continued down the hall. I counted four bedrooms. How many guests did he expect to have at once? They were opulent rooms, too. Huge king size mattresses on four poster beds, the kind with the curtains.

Why did he have rooms that looked like they belonged to Ebenezer Scrooge?

I could hear laughter coming from the kitchen when I walked back by it. Good to know they found something funny as long as I wasn't in the room with them.

I went back to the living room and curled up in the corner of a couch. I counted the number of books on the bookcases but lost count about halfway down the wall. I was tired and scared, and I wanted this to all be over.

I could feel the tears start, and I swiped at my face. I didn't want Greg to know I had been crying again. We were somewhere safe for now, and acting like a blubbering mess wasn't going to help the situation. I couldn't go to him for comfort anyway; it was my own fault I had opened a gulf between us. I had been shoving and resisting everything he had offered me from the start, and the moment I had an offer from him I wanted, I flung it back in his face.

But I had heard guilt in his voice when Patrice had come up. I had to wonder if his interest in me was because he saw someone he could rescue, unlike how he had apparently failed her, or felt he did.

I settled my head on the arm of the couch and stared at

the wall of books until I fell asleep.

I woke up briefly when I felt someone lift me. I was cradled against someone's chest, and he smelled like lemons. I snuggled into him and went back to sleep.

∞

I was back at the party.

Things were going fine until someone handed me some pills and a cup of beer.

And I had been stupid enough to take them.

Everything had gotten blurry and kind of disconnected. Like I wasn't quite attached to my body anymore and I was standing with the figures and the whispers in whatever space it is they go to when I'm not actively calling them to me.

Then someone was pulling me up the stairs towards the bedrooms, and I was telling him no, and he wasn't listening, and the shadows were *hungry*.

So, I let them out.

There was so much screaming.

And so much blood.

By the time it stopped, there was no way to tell what color anything had been before it was painted red.

There was still screaming. But I was the only living thing in that house.

∞

I sat up, lunged for the edge of the bed, and retched. And then retched again. Until the contents of my stomach were strewn over the Persian rug the bed was placed on. And then I lay there, panting, trying to figure out how I was going to tell

Virgil I was not paying for that.

The door to the room was cracked, and light from the hallway was spilling in. I could hear murmurs.

Carefully, I eased out of bed, making sure not to step in the vomit. I wanted water so I could wash my mouth out, and I would have to pass back into the living room to get to a bathroom. The kitchen was closer.

Quietly, I padded down the hallway. I was going to have to go by the security room to get to the kitchen. Inside, I saw Greg and Virgil, both focused on the monitors. I paused, just outside the door, vacillating: kitchen or eavesdrop? I chose to eavesdrop.

What? Just because I made comments about Greg doing it doesn't mean I'm not above doing it myself. Especially when I know someone has hidden information from me before. Regardless of whatever his intentions might be.

"What is he doing?" Greg was asking.

"He's just prowling in circles around my property. Like he's trying to sniff something out."

The monitors were glowing green, and I could see the shape of something dog-like pass by the camera. My stomach lurched again. Greg turned.

"Meg. Jesus, Meg, are you okay?" And he was striding toward me, and I backed away. He stopped.

"I'm sorry," I said, my voice hoarse. "I just, I need some water."

And then he was there, one warm arm slung around my shoulders and was gently leading me to the kitchen. "Sit," he said, settling me on a stool. He set two glasses in front of me, one full of water, the other empty. "Rinse and spit," he said. I did as he instructed, and when I was done, he removed both the glasses and set one full of clean water in front of me. He waited, watching me until I had downed half of it. Then he sat down on the stool next to me.

"Are you okay?" he repeated.

"Nightmare," I said. "Um, Virgil's gonna need to get his rug cleaned. I can't pay for that."

"Just blame his cooking," Greg said.

I gave him a weak smile.

His hand was rubbing circles on my back, and I stared at the glass of water in my hands. I sniffed, tears springing back to the corners of my eyes. I twitched my shoulders. I needed him to stop touching me, or I would start crying and wouldn't be able to stop.

His hand stilled, and he watched me silently. I sniffled again, turning my face away from him.

"Do you need my shirt?" he asked.

The dam broke. I sobbed, twisting my body away from his, head in my hands while I furiously tried to wipe away the tears, but they just kept coming. He got up from his stool and came around to face me, pulling me against his chest, his nose in my hair again.

"Shhhhh," he whispered. His lips were pressed against the top of my head. "Shhhh."

"I'm sorry," I sobbed against him, but I couldn't have said what I was apologizing for. There were too many things in that instant that the guilt and penance could have been for. "I'm sorry."

He just tightened his arms around me and let me cry.

I lifted my head up when the tears finally slowed. I tried to push away, and he loosened his arms but didn't let go of me. Instead, he used his thumb to wipe tears off my face.

"Are you okay?" he asked.

"It was just a stupid nightmare," I said.

"It feels like it might have been more than that," he said, looking me in the eye.

I didn't answer him, because how was I supposed to explain it? Instead, I looked down at the floor.

"Meg," he sighed. "Could you just talk to me? As a friend?"

Except I didn't want to talk about it with anyone. How could I explain it anyway? What the whispers and I were? What we had done? So I reverted to my age-old response of anger and biting sarcasm, except when I looked back up at him, the retort died on my lips. He looked so worried, and it made me want to reassure him that I was fine. I think we must have moved at the same time because then his lips were on mine, and he pulled me off the stool against him and I could feel the hard line of his body pressed against mine. I wanted to drown in that feeling.

Someone cleared their throat. We sprang apart.

Virgil was standing in the doorway. "Ahem. He can come over the fence, and he flew in too low for the guns to be able to hit him. For future reference for you, Gregor, shitty sedans not needed. He is currently attempting to open the front door. Thought you might want to know. But, you know, it's locked, and there's no exterior handle, so…as you were." And he walked away.

I felt my face redden. Greg's lips were pressed together in a grim line. "Him and his goddamn timing."

I switched subjects. "How does Virgil get into his house if the door doesn't have a handle?"

Greg scrubbed at his face. "He's telekinetic. He doesn't need the door to have a handle." He started to steer me toward the door. "Here, I'm putting you in my room."

I balked, digging my heels into the floor.

Greg looked into my face. "I will sleep on the floor if you want me to, but I am not leaving you separated from me right now."

"You're taking this 'protect Meg at all costs' thing really seriously," I grumbled. But I let him lead me to one of the other bedrooms. Fortunately, he let me climb into the bed on my own or he would've been sleeping outside the door. I don't care what he said about not being separated.

I busied myself for a moment setting up a line of pillows down the middle of the bed. I pointed. "You can sleep there." Then I flopped down onto the pillow I had kept for my head, pulling the blankets up under my chin.

He chuckled but settled himself on the bed, back resting against the headboard, legs stretched out along the mattress. He crossed his arms. He put his chin down. "Try to get some rest, Meg."

CHAPTER EIGHT

When I woke up, Greg had slumped over at some point in the night, his head resting on the pillow next to mine. I don't know how he managed to keep his arms crossed over his chest in that position, though. I slid off the bed and padded out of the room, down the hallway and to the kitchen. Virgil was already there, and when I saw him, I almost turned tail back out the door.

"You don't have to be scared of me," he said. "Come, have some coffee."

"I'm not scared of you," I said, still poised by the door.

"Then sit down," he said, sliding a full mug over in front of the stool I had occupied the day before.

I hesitated, still on the threshold. He simply waited, leaning back against the counter by the coffee pot, taking sips out of his mug. His eyes watched me. I took an experimental step forward, and when he didn't move, crossed the rest of the space and sat down, pulling the mug he had set down the rest of the way over.

"Tell me about yourself, Meg," he said.

"There isn't anything to tell," I said to him, chin raised.

There was a glint of amusement in his eyes. "I feel like there's a lot to tell."

"Well, you won't hear any of it from me."

"Hmm," he said. "Generally, people like talking about themselves."

I shrugged. I'm not saying I'm different from most people when it comes to that. I just didn't want to talk about me with him.

What? I've been talking to you, haven't I?

And something was bothering me. "Why didn't you tell Greg about the anti-aircraft guns not being able to aim low sooner?"

"Hmm, he wouldn't have cared previously," Virgil turned, poured himself more coffee. "But then, he's never had a passenger with him before. Usually, he comes in alone. I don't think I've ever actually hit him, but I suppose, if he was bringing a guest, he didn't want to chance it."

I stared at him, mildly horrified. "You mean you actually shoot at him?"

"I have a callbox for a reason."

"I thought you were friends."

"We are."

"But you shoot at him?"

"We can go around in this circle all day and my answer will be the same. I have a callbox for a reason."

I was still having trouble processing that. I mean, Greg had warned me that Virgil would shoot at him, but I didn't realize it was a common occurrence between the two of them.

"Ah, where are my manners? Would you like some breakfast? I have bacon. Just don't tell Gregor."

My stomach rumbled, making the decision for me. "Yes," I said.

Virgil busied himself pulling things out of the fridge: butter, eggs, buttermilk, bacon. He turned to a cabinet, pulled out flour, salt, honey, baking powder. What was he doing?

I watched him measuring, dumping things into a bowl. The eggs and bacon remained untouched. "What are you doing?"

"Making biscuits," he said. Like I should somehow know that. But I wasn't sure how to respond without sounding offended, so I kept my mouth shut. I know, it was a Herculean feat for me not to make some sort of snarky comment. I think I strained something. So instead, I watched him as he flattened out the dough and then cut biscuits out, placing them into a cast iron pan he had magicked out of some cabinet somewhere.

"Your coffee is going to get cold," he told me.

I took a sip and regretted it. The coffee was already cold, but I choked it down because I wasn't going to admit it to him. But from the way his lips twitched, and the corner of his eyes crinkled, he already knew.

"Would you like a fresh cup?" he asked. "Although I'll have to make another pot if we're going to save any for Gregor."

"No," I said. He met my eyes, and he looked like he was measuring whether to call me on the lie. He leaned over the counter and pulled the mug back toward him, out of my reach. Dumped the coffee in the sink and poured me another cup before placing it back in front of me and turned to set up the pot to brew again.

He had moved on to the eggs and bacon now that the biscuits were in the oven, using separate pans for them. His movements through the kitchen were sparse but fluid. Without Greg in the room, he seemed content to keep to himself rather than verbally spar with me. I couldn't tell if he had sensed and was trying to respect my need for space or if it was because it was that awkward silence between two people who barely know each other and now find themselves forced to socialize without the bridge who had introduced them.

He had set down a plate in front of me before he spoke to me again. "When exactly did he first show interest in you that you're aware of?"

"Who?" I asked startled. "Greg?"

There was a flicker in his eyes that I wasn't sure how to read. I wouldn't have called it amusement, more like he was pleased with something. "No," he said slowly. "Red Eye. When was the first time you became aware of his interest in you?"

"Greg didn't tell you already?"

"He has told me what he knows. I want to hear it from you."

"Why?"

Virgil regarded me seriously, his expression stern. "Because the more information I have the more help I can be."

"He showed up outside my bedroom window," I said after a moment of quiet consideration on whether I wanted to answer. But I could be hamstringing myself if I didn't.

"What day was that?" Virgil asked.

I had to pause to think about it. I had to think back to when I had coffee with Greg. Friday - Saturday he showed up at my job, then, how many nights later?

"Wednesday night," I finally said. Because I had been scheduled for closing that Thursday.

"The next time?"

"Thursday night."

"Back to Wednesday, what did he do?"

"I already told all this to Greg—"

"Humor me."

I scowled at him. "He licked the window and told me to scare him, so I did." I waited, expecting Virgil to ask the same question Greg had asked me: why I would listen to some random demon creature when it told me it wanted me to scare it? But Virgil didn't say anything, he just waited.

Finally, he sighed. "And? Did anything else occur? Was that the first time he turned your power back on you?"

"Yes." Since he seemed to be waiting again, I answered the unspoken questions. "I didn't get hurt. I just let the power go and he left."

"And Thursday night? What occurred then?"

"He broke into my apartment through the sliding glass doors to the balcony. I called Greg while he was—" I paused to take a breath, because the memory of it made my heart pound. "He was pushing on the glass, like, like he wanted to - like he thought this was a fucking horror movie."

"What form was he in?"

"He looked like a dog. Wait, Thursday morning! He was human, and he showed up at the coffee shop when I stopped by."

"The next time?" And so, Virgil's grilling went on. Through my, escape, from Greg's apartment down to when Red Eye had shown up outside Greg's apartment that next night. He brought me back around to the first event, asking for his exact wording. He asked about what he said outside the coffee shop, at the internet café. What did the messages he left say? He kept making me repeat them, picking apart the details, what there was of them.

He didn't leave off his questioning until Greg appeared in the kitchen doorway.

"Well, good morning. I see you've decided to join us,"

Virgil said.

"Morning," Greg grunted, helping himself to coffee, and looking at the eggs and bacon. "Did you cook those in butter or fat?"

"Butter," Virgil said.

"Thanks," Greg grunted again, helping himself to what was left of the eggs. He brought his plate and mug around and sat next to me. His leg brushed against mine. I left my leg where it was.

What? I was here first, he's in my space. If he has a problem with it, he can move.

"Meg and I were just having a chat about her little problem."

Greg paused in his eating to shoot Virgil a look. "*Little* problem?"

"Yes. Little. The size isn't important. What is important is how he's finding her."

"You have a theory?" Greg picked up his mug, taking a sip before he went back to eating.

"It's the second message that has me curious. Why her dreams?"

"That's not a theory."

"It's the start of one."

"Which is?"

"What kind of dreams do you have, Meg?" Virgil said, turning his attention back to me.

The muscles in my back and shoulders tensed, and I stared back at him. "Just dreams." *Liar*, the whispers sighed in my ears. It made me jerk.

Virgil was studying me, and Greg had straightened up, half turned toward me.

"Meg?" he said.

My head was tilted, trying to hear what the whispers wanted to say, but it was too late, it had faded. Only the feeling of disapproval remained. From the whispers or the look Virgil was giving me, I wasn't sure. I was balanced on another precipice, where I had to choose.

"Why does the type of dream matter?" I finally asked, trying to delay the moment.

"I won't know if the type matters without knowing what you dream about," Virgil said.

Greg shifted next to me again, his leg rubbing against mine, and I focused on that. "Nightmares," I said.

"About any event in particular? Or are they the typical kinds, naked at work, falling?"

I met Virgil's eyes; my lips pressed together because I didn't want to say. For a moment, I wished he could read my mind because maybe if I could tell him without saying it out loud, I wouldn't have to answer any more questions about it.

"I see," Virgil said, although I don't know how he could. "I have some research I need to do," he said, and he left the kitchen.

Greg and I were left at the island, his leg still pressed against mine. "You alright?" he asked me.

"Fine," I said, although I wasn't sure if I was. Virgil's questioning could put you through the wringer. He hadn't been as mercurial as he had been the night before, and I was left feeling confused.

He was watching me again. "You get used to him," he told me.

"I'm not sure I want to," I said.

Greg chuckled and then kissed my head. The casual affection made me start.

Look, I know his leg was there, and that sort of counts,

but this is still different.

He coughed and cleared his throat; he must have heard the way my heart jumped with me. "Sorry," he said.

I took the leap. "Don't be."

He smiled at me. I leaned forward, brushing his lips with mine. His response was instantaneous; he came up off his stool, one hand in my hair, the other on my back, my head tilted up. His touch - soft, tender, light and fleeting - left me wanting more. But he pulled back, his hand on my face, thumb stroking my cheek.

"Meg," he said. "You don't owe me anything."

The confusion must have shown on my face. Although I suppose I don't have a good poker face anyway and probably wouldn't have been able to cover it.

He made a frustrated noise. "For last night. For any help you've been willing to take from me. You don't owe me anything for that."

"Why would you think I think I owe you?" I demanded.

"You—" and he stopped, scrubbing at his face. "You confuse me."

"You and me both," I said.

It surprised a laugh out of him. But he sobered quickly. "I don't want you to feel pushed into whatever this thing is, between us."

"I don't let anyone push me anywhere," I said.

"I've noticed," he said dryly.

"Then why would you think I feel obligated to you in some way?" Because he hadn't answered my question.

He was silent, staring into my eyes, and I was going to need to either move away or step forward, because the tension between us had changed. I needed him to say something because I was afraid I would make the wrong choice. And for him not to say anything, because what if it was something I didn't want to hear? My heart was thumping against my chest; there was no way he couldn't hear it. I would never be able to keep a secret from him if I took this path. I would need him not to keep secrets from me.

His hand hadn't moved from my face, but the silence was stretching, straining. And I needed an answer.

"Why?" I asked again.

"My apartment, you had just lost your job—"

"I don't—"

"The field, you point blank said you didn't want—"

"That wasn't—"

"Here you just had a, I don't know, whatever it was, more than a nightmare—"

"It wasn't—"

"This morning, I don't know what this is. Your heart speeds up in a good way, when I'm near you, but the moment I touch you, you jerk away from me."

"There're different speeds?" I asked, distracted.

"Yes," he said, and I couldn't tell if he was impatient or not. "There's different speeds between fear, lying, exertion, joy or sorrow. They feel similar, but I can hear the difference in the beat. The breath. The vessels and the way the blood moves. Your body language doesn't always match what I'm hearing. I don't know what you want."

It sounded like a dizzying amount of information to process, but it also didn't sound like the subject he wanted to be discussing at the moment.

"How do you know what anyone wants?" I was procrastinating, stretching it out.

"Part of it is reading them; part of it is intuiting what I hear. Generally, I'm pretty good at figuring out what they're after."

"Have you ever been wrong?" I was thinking back to what he had said to me about his instincts regarding people when he came by looking for lightbulbs.

"Not yet," he said.

Well, he was going to be wrong about me. Being a villain takes too much effort anyway.

"What do you want, Meg?" he asked me.

I was in a marsh, and one wrong step would land me in quicksand. "What do you want?" I asked him, a question for a question.

He was exasperated. I could see it in his face. "No, I'm not answering that. I want you to tell me what you want, not what you think I want to hear from you."

"I mean, there's an equal amount of chance that I would just tell you the opposite of what you want to hear just to piss you off so…" I said, and trailed off, because he hadn't even cracked a grin at that.

I don't do well with serious conversations. I mean, I might lead us headlong into one, but the moment things get too significant, I do my absolute best to back the fuck out.

Maybe I would do better if I told him what I didn't need and let him figure it out on his own.

"I don't need a protector," I finally said. "Or a handler, or a fucking guardian."

"An equal?"

"Yes," I said. I wanted an equal.

"Because you can rescue yourself."

"Yes."

He was thinking, his eyes still steady on mine, and I didn't know how I'd managed to go this long with his hand on my face because anyone else I'd have been screaming at to get out of my space.

Or, you know, would've murdered them by now.

He took a breath, "Do you think I could be that equal?"

"Yes," I said, my heart hammering because now I had jumped off that precipice, leapt for the safety of an unknown bank in that marsh.

He kissed me, and in that moment my heart soared, his arms tightening around me. My hands rested against his chest, inching their way up. He pulled back before I was ready, resting his forehead against mine.

"Virgil'll be back any minute," he said, "and as much as I want to, if we keep going—" He stopped. I was tempted to keep going anyway. His room wasn't that far from the kitchen. But he was straightening, loosening his arms from around me. "Come on," he said, "We'll go watch TV. I might let you convince me to watch a musical."

"Hmm, no, you wasted your chance," I told him.

"One chance? I got one chance?" he said. "You don't think that's kind of harsh?"

"Nope," I said, hopping off the stool. "I don't make the rules."

"You know, I feel like that's not entirely accurate," he said, an echo of an earlier conversation.

"Hmm, maybe I make some of the rules," I said. He chuckled, and it made me feel warm.

∞

At some point Virgil came sailing out of wherever he had disappeared to. When he found us on the couch watching TV, he walked by, making the screen black with a flick of his hand. Greg had half thrown his hands up.

"We were watching that," he said.

"I can turn it back on. Or you can listen," Virgil said, although he didn't look like he was planning on discussing anything quite yet, because he was making his way down his bookshelves, pulling books off the shelf.

"What did you find?" Greg asked.

"Lots of things. It's just a question of which one is the right one."

"Riddles," Greg said.

"That is not a riddle." Virgil dumped the books on the coffee table and was leaning over it, flipping through the pages of one.

"It's not an explanation either," countered Greg.

"I am *looking*," said Virgil emphasizing the word, "for any heroes or villains in all the old tales that could explain, or give us an idea, of how Red Eye is doing what he does. We don't have enough information from his previous kills."

Greg had straightened up, pulling his arm out from behind my back. "Meaning?"

"We don't know what he's doing in terms of tracking them before he kills them," Virgil said, like it was obvious. "Is he tracking them the same way he's tracking Meg? Is there a correlation between her nightmares and him being present?"

Greg had relaxed, leaning forward, elbows on his knees. "So, what did you find?"

Virgil had opened another book and was turning the pages on that one, the first still open and set aside. "So far in the running for consideration and further research we have the Mare, a Baku, Pesanta, Ogun Oru, the Alu, Phobetor or the god Epiales, son of—"

"Nyx," I said. Virgil looked up from the book, focusing on me. I might have sunk back into the couch. Being Virgil's singular focus was disquieting.

"What can you tell me about Epiales and Phobetor, Meg?"

"Anything I could tell you, you can find on the internet," I said.

"Humor me," he said. Must be a favorite phrase of his.

"There isn't much to tell," I warned him.

"Kind of like you?"

"They were both the sons of Nyx," I said, skipping past Virgil's dig. "Supposedly Phobetor would appear in nightmares, but Epiales could make them come true. Sometimes it seems like there's not a consensus on whether they were the same or separate. And there was a third brother. All part of the Oneiroi."

"And the third?"

"Morpheus. But some of this information comes from Ovid, so—" I shrugged. It was the best I could do, and I could be misremembering anyway. There was a lot of information I had shoved away to the back of my head to try and forget it, and now I was having to dust it off.

Virgil's hand was at his chin as he slowly turned pages on yet another book. "So, we have tales of monsters and men who had power related to dreams and nightmares. And they either caused them with their presence or entered ones already in progress."

I was silent because I didn't know if Virgil wanted a response to that.

"But it doesn't explain—" he said, stopping, and I watched his eyes moving back and forth as he read through the page he was on. "Is he tracking her through the dreams or something else?" he muttered to himself. One finger moved down the page before he flipped to the next. He seemed to have forgotten we were in the room.

When he did finally look up, he focused on Greg. "When you found Patrice, where was she?"

Greg shoved his hair back. "Her home."

"Her lair, you mean. Villains live in lairs," Virgil said, his eyes and voice steady.

"I'm not going to argue the semantics with you," Greg said, his tone biting. "It was her home."

"And she was alone?"

"You know she was."

Virgil was making what I was quickly beginning to consider his thinking face, his hand back up at his chin. "Was her lair set apart from any other residences? No neighbors?"

"You know the answer to that, too," Greg said.

"Remind me," Virgil said, still cool and clinical.

"Yes."

"How many other villains are you aware of that he's taken down?"

"Five," Greg said, meaning a grand total of six. It doesn't seem like many, but when you take into account there's only a few hundred people with powers in a world of billions, and only so many of them are actually, well, "out," that total can add up quickly. Most people have small powers. A little extra strength there, some extra luck here.

Those of us who are truly dangerous to the population at large, we're even fewer. Which is good for the normal people.

But what's not good is when you have a singular villain picking off other powerful people and no idea what his motivation is. And it was no wonder he had been operating without detection. The villains don't talk much to each other, and who's going to care if they die anyway? The only time I've heard of them caring about anything is when one of them tries to retire. Apparently, there's no such thing as retiring from villain life. You either die, or, well, you can't quit, so you die. It just depends on how long it takes them to catch up to you.

Look, I don't make these rules. You would think they would be cool with that kind of decrease in the competition.

Don't ask me why they tried to recruit me either. The only thing I can think of is they just didn't want another hero out there mucking up their plans for world domination.

"You're missing information on two," Virgil said.

Oh. Eight. Eight victims.

"How long has he been doing this?" I asked. Because eight seemed high. Why are you going to argue this with me? How many do you think it needs to be before it's a high number?

"A year that we're aware of," Virgil said.

"A year? Eight in a year?" I squeaked. And then had to clear my throat. Eight villains in a year, and they're not soft targets, not if they're known as villains. I'm not kidding when I say we're all dangerous. Some of you have no idea what the veneer of society is hiding from you.

Although now I could understand all the caution surrounding when and where to go after him. If Greg had been aware of six, that alone would be enough to give any hero pause.

"Yes, eight as far as we know," Virgil said. The implication that there could be more was clear.

Greg had half turned, putting a hand on my back. "He's not getting that count any higher."

Virgil was watching us again. "Hmm," he said. "You said you lived in an apartment, Meg?"

"Yes."

"What was he planning to do about the attention that

would attract?" Virgil half muttered to himself.

"Maybe he's escalating and didn't plan ahead?" I asked. Serial killers do that, right? They get too comfortable, or too focused on the hunt and start slipping and making mistakes. That's how they usually get caught, isn't it?

Look, I don't watch murder shows. I watch fun shit. I've been around enough death; I don't need it for entertainment too. Get out of here with your *Tiger King* and *Cecil Hotel* and *Unsolved Mysteries*.

What I do know is that eventually, even the villains he's going after won't be enough for him. And I might be that steppingstone.

"Or he's escalating in terms of his methods," Virgil said. "But he would've had to—" he paused again. "I need a map," he said. "What's near your apartment, Meg? Anything abandoned? In development?"

"I don't know," I told him. "I go to work, I go home. Sometimes I venture far enough to get food."

Greg snorted.

Virgil focused on me again. "Think. How do you get to work?"

"The bus."

"What does it pass? Which streets does it take? Do you take the same route home?"

"I—" I had to pause to think about it. I don't pay a whole lot of attention to my surroundings. I mean, I know I should, vulnerable-looking woman all on her own. The fact that I'm alone would be enough encouragement for your run-of-the-mill predators to take their chances.

But I don't because I've never been vulnerable like this before. Even if my sense of safety with my home wasn't quite where it used to be, my confidence that I could handle whatever got thrown at me was the same as it ever was. Anyone who tried to take me down would die, and that was the end of it.

Red Eye had shoved me into entirely new territory, and I didn't like it.

I was frustrated and angry - at myself for never paying attention, at Virgil for inadvertently pointing that out to me, at this stupid fucking demon creature for screwing up the way things had been going. I mean, yeah, it wasn't some amazing or great life, but I had things where I wanted them. It had been smooth for the most part, even if it was mediocre. I knew what to expect. Work, home, frozen foods, hero recruitments where I would tell them to fuck off.

Quiet. As normal as it could be for someone like me.

And I took that out on Virgil. "Why does that even matter?" I finally snapped at him. "What does it matter where I fucking went? What was around me? Who cares!"

He didn't back down. His expression didn't change, stoic and unwavering. "I care," he said, "because I want to know what he was planning to do and how he was planning to do it. The where and the why. Is there something about you that's different from his other victims? What is it? To understand him, I need to understand his motivations. What more is there that we're missing?"

"I don't think Meg can answer those questions," Greg said. There was an air of warning in his voice, but I didn't know who the warning was directed at or what it was about.

But Virgil seemed to know. He switched his eyes to Greg, and his look was considering. "I see," Virgil said. I don't know what he saw in that moment. The tone seemed so unrelated to what we had been discussing. "Meg, if you will give me your address, I will pull up the satellite images and see if I can find anything relevant, and *inform*," again the emphasis on a single word, "you of any if so."

"1100 Black Bear Creek, apartment 3 B, Malus City," I told him.

"Thank you," Virgil said, and he left us on the couch. I heard a door down the hallway slam.

Greg was scrubbing at his face.

"What?" I asked him. He looked irritated.

"Nothing," he said. "Virgil - sometimes dealing with him is frustrating."

"He's your friend," I pointed out.

"I am aware of that, yes." Greg settled back into the couch, his hand still on my back. "Did you want to go back to the TV or find something else for entertainment?"

"We could always be old-fashioned and talk to each other."

Greg chuckled. "You going to tell me your deepest, darkest secrets?"

"You going to tell me yours?"

He switched topics, dodging the subject. "Other than watching musicals, what do you do?"

"Read," I said, answering him instead of pushing the matter. If his secrets were anything like mine, they weren't really secrets. Just a past written down in some government file somewhere that we would prefer not to remember.

"You didn't have many books in your apartment."

"Libraries exist for a reason."

Also, I have the internet. I don't participate in social media, but I scroll through it. Memes, gifs, reddit - I'm a pop culture connoisseur with a magpie-like tendency to collect random bits of information.

I mean, I don't use it all that often. But the information is there. I even know some fancy words, too. I do more than just sprinkle swear words into everyday conversation, although that is a special kind of gift all on its own. You should try it sometime; it might improve your mood.

But our conversation had stuttered to a halt. Greg seemed like he was debating whether to continue the current line of questioning or find a new subject.

And I'm allowed to ask questions too. "So, how many cars did you steal as a teenager?" What? That's not a deep, dark secret; we already touched on this subject.

"No comment," he said.

"Of the unknown number of cars you stole, how many did you wreck?"

His lips were twitching. "What makes you think I wrecked them?"

"I mean, you sure seemed to know a lot about what would happen to me if you wrecked that sedan so-"

"You know, I don't think I like where this line of questioning is going."

"You could just answer the question to start with, and then maybe the line wouldn't go somewhere you don't want it to."

"You say that, but I don't believe you."

"Not my fault you're such a suspecting person."

"When I can hear you lying, it's hard not to be."

We were back to that. Would all our conversations end in hero talk? He straightened up again, looking down into my face.

"What?" he asked.

"Is it always like this?" He waited, and I wondered if he was thinking or waiting for me to clarify what I meant. And I can only stand to let the silence stretch for so long. So, I gave a helpless kind of wave at the room. "This. Is the hero thing just

. . . always there?"

"Yes," he said, cautious, like he wasn't sure where this was about to go but suspected that it was a place he had been before and didn't want to be there again.

"Okay," I said.

"Okay?" he asked.

"Okay," I said.

"That's it?" he asked. "No issue with that? You don't have a problem with the hero thing always being on?"

"Why would I?"

I think I had managed to stump him, that he was expecting some kind of protest. Some kind of objection to always returning to the subject.

Look, I know what I said about heroes. I'm allowed to grow as a person. Plus, half my problem with them would've been solved if they would've left me alone. You'd be pissed off at the whole lot of them too.

He leaned back again, and he looked like he was brooding, so it was my turn. "What?" I asked.

"You wouldn't let me fly you anywhere until you had no choice," he said.

"Yeah, because I don't want people to know what I am or be a hero. I like the quiet life."

"Life with me around isn't going to be quiet," he said, sounding apprehensive.

"Are you going to expect me to go save the world?" I asked.

"No."

"Then we'll get along just fine. You go do what you want, and I'll do what I want."

"No villainy," he said. "Firm rule."

"No villainy," I agreed. "That's too much work

anyway."

CHAPTER NINE

We had ended up back in the kitchen, trying to figure out lunch. Greg was reluctant to go anywhere to start with, since Red Eye had been haunting the grounds the night before. So even if we didn't want what was available, we weren't sure we wanted to chance it.

We ended up settling for peanut butter and jelly sandwiches because it was the easiest solution. Also, I might have badgered Greg into something other than salad.

When Virgil came in, the look on his face convinced me we didn't want to try leaving. "That fucking thing is still hovering around. He's staying off the fence, and he's just circling again." He sounded offended.

I set my sandwich down, suddenly not hungry. Greg's hand was on my back again. I changed my focus. "You have any soda?" I asked. "I didn't see any in the fridge."

"No," Virgil said. "Sugar's horrible for you."

No soda was such a small thing to be upset about in that moment. But I was tired of the questioning, I was tired of being hunted, and I was tired of being tired. I got up, knocking the stool over and stormed out of the kitchen, hesitating in the hallway. Which room?

I ended up heading for the room I had started in the night before. I could always change my mind.

Someone had cleaned the rug; I could see that as soon as I walked in. And there were only two options as to who it had been since it wasn't me.

I slammed the door behind me and locked it. The gesture might have been futile because I was currently caged with a telekinetic and a strong man. I doubted the flimsy lock on that door could keep either of them out if they wanted to get in.

Silence.

The whispers came to me, sighing in my ears, fingers ruffling my hair and sliding against my skin. Their touch was cool. It was always cool. We moved away from the door. If I kept them close to me, an aura of shadow, anyone else would be well out of the range of their compulsion. And it would let me take a minute to breathe.

You would think I would hate them for being what they are, but I can't. They're a part of me, and I think I gave up punishing myself a while ago.

The guilt won't leave though.

So we stood there, the whispers, the figures, the shadows and I, in our own little corner of our own little room. Until there was a knock at the door. The whispers vanished, leaving the air warmer than it had been while they were here.

I hesitated against the wall opposite the door.

They knocked again. "Meg? Can I come in?" Greg's voice.

I crossed the room, unlocked the door and stepped back.

"Is that a yes?" Greg asked.

I rolled my eyes but turned the knob so that that door

cracked open and stepped back again.

Greg pushed the door open, poking his head and shoulders in. "I don't know if that's an answer."

"I wouldn't have unlocked the door if I didn't want you to come in," I told him.

He came the rest of the way in, shutting the door behind him. "Are you okay?" he asked.

"It's just a soda," I said.

"Hmm," he said. I realized we would have a lot of moments where he would have to decide if he would call me on a lie. He was watching me with those dark eyes. "We'll find a solution," he said.

"I know," I said, although I wasn't sure which one of us was lying now. What if there wasn't a solution? Would I spend the rest of my life trapped in Virgil's compound?

He had stepped away from the door, coming up to me, a hand on the back of my neck, his fingers so warm compared to the figures. He bent his face to mine and kissed me.

And I was rising up on my toes, my arms sliding up to twine around his neck. Because as gentle as he was, I was on fire with need.

Look, it's been a while, okay. Keep your comments to yourself.

He had wrapped one arm around my waist, and I could feel his fingers flex against my hip. His other hand had migrated up into my hair. And still his lips were soft and slow, the light brush of his fingers sliding against my skin as his hand moved up my back, slipping under my shirt. I trembled. He had moved his hand from my hair, and I wanted to demand he put it back. Except then it was under my shirt with his other hand.

"Meg," he said.

I couldn't catch my breath, the feel of his hands against my ribs, inching higher, making me gasp.

He pulled back. "Jesus, wait, Meg." His voice was hoarse, his breathing ragged.

"For what?" I demanded. I'm not fucking waiting!

"I wasn't planning on this."

"I literally do not care what the plan was. I want this. Do you?"

"Yes, that's not—"

"Then what is?"

"Protection," he said.

"IUD," I countered. "Tested for STDs, all clear." And plus, long dry spell between the last one and this, so it's been a while. Not that that's any of his business.

Look, I'm a responsible adult about the things that I think matter. Not getting pregnant and safe sex is one of them. You can judge me over that all you want. At least I know how to have fun. Safe fun. Shut up.

He was studying me. "I can't. I can't get tested."

"Why not?" Like, that would definitely be a deal breaker if he's out there bare backing it with everyone.

He cleared his throat. "They can't draw my blood; needles can't get through my skin."

"What do they do if you get sick?"

"It's never been a problem."

"You've never been sick?"

"No."

"Some people have all the luck," I muttered.

He chuckled. One hand on my face, his thumb stroking my cheek again. "I've been safe about it," he said, "but I'm not moving forward with you because I don't have any condoms on me. And I'm not going to do anything we're not both comfortable with."

I kind of wanted to break something. And he saw it.

"Hold on," he said, giving me a kiss and then leaving the room. I think the temperature dropped; at least, I certainly felt colder without his arms around me.

He had slipped back into the room with a box.

"Where-" I started, "You know what, I don't want to know where," I said. "But I do want to know: that many, huh?" Because I did not want to know if he just went and asked Virgil for some. Especially if Virgil's response was to hand him an entire box. Although maybe Virgil is into the whole boy scout spiel thing, you know, always be prepared?

Yeah, I don't want to be thinking about Virgil right now either.

Greg chuckled and tossed the box onto the bed. He was slipping his hands back up my shirt, his lips on my neck, moving up, his breath in my ear. "Where were we?"

"Further than that," I said.

His hands skimmed down. "Here?"

"Uh uh," I said, although he had one hand down the back of my pants now. His lips were on mine, a hand in my hair.

And this time I pulled back, so I could get my shirt off. His lips went lower, on my neck, my shoulders, my collarbone. He had slid his hand back out of my pants, lifted me up and onto the bed, settled me on my back. His lips were skimming down my body, his breath tickling, warm against my skin.

He came back up, his lips back on mine again, and he had lost his shirt at some point. I hadn't noticed when he took it off. The feel of his skin against mine, his hands slipping down, he shifted, his hands in the waistband of my jeans, and he was peeling them off, achingly slow.

His breath was back in my ear, his body pressed against mine. "Meg," he said. My heart fluttered.

It was the only word he said for a while after that.

∞

I was in the house again.

But strangely, this time it was empty. The dream, the nightmare, had changed.

I stood in the living room, slowly turning. Where was everyone?

I should be relieved, but this difference, it made me nervous.

Then the walls started dripping blood.

Oh good, when did this become *Poltergeist*? Or was it *The Shining*? No, that one had an elevator of blood. Both could be the wrong movie, but it doesn't really matter, does it? I don't do horror.

Also, if someone's trying to scare me, they're going to need to a do a better job than that. I've been covered in so much blood and gore it was hard to tell where the gore ended and I began. I had been bathed in blood by the time I was sixteen, and it had continued past that.

If you're going to walk by yourself at night, make sure you're the biggest predator out there. And don't run into me.

Mirage might have been the only villain I took out, but there were others who thought I was prey. Before I had settled into my life here, that is, because that's when I stopped going out at night altogether.

But before - maybe I was daring them to come after me.

But we're still in my dream right now, and the blood is still running down the walls, and pooling on the floor. I was getting less impressed by the minute. What kind of B movie production is this? At least be original.

I stood there and watched the blood slowly creeping toward my shoes.

Until the hands came out.

They were reaching up out of the blood, sinew, muscle and bone, skin hanging in shreds from the fingers and arms.

Those made me back up real quick.

I bumped into someone behind me.

You know that expression the about-to-die ditz makes when she realizes the killer has been in the house the whole time?

I know, I just became a horror movie cliché. Because that was absolutely my face. Down to the slow, oh fuck, this isn't good turn.

"Hello, little lady," he purred at me, white teeth bared in that monstrous grin.

I screamed.

∞

"Meg! MEG!" Someone was bellowing my name.

The whispers, figures and shadows were swirling around me, creating their own wind, so agitated was their passage through the air. They were ruffling the curtains, the sheets and blankets half dragged off the bed, like someone had surged up out of it in a hurry.

"Meg!" I looked over at the voice. Greg was pressed back against the wall by the door, as far as he could get from me in the room without leaving.

"Sorry," I whispered. The whispers settled against my shoulders, figures curling against my arms. Greg stayed against

141

the wall. The whispers were sighing in my ears; the danger was past, and they could go, but they stayed, fingers pressing against my skin.

"Meg," Greg said slowly, "I can't get near you until they go."

"How many of them can you see?" I asked, delaying, because I could feel the shadows looming at my back. They were restless for a reason, and I wasn't sure I wanted to know what for.

"Three," Greg said. "At least, I think it's three."

"What do they look like to you?"

He was studying me. I could see the way his muscles were clenched, the way his hands were shaking. "*This* is an important question right now?" he asked me.

"I have to be calm enough to let them go," I said. A half-truth, enough that he might not hear the lie. Because right now I wasn't sure they would listen when I told them they could leave.

"Okay," he said. He stayed where he was, but I could see the way his eyes roved over us. "Shadows at the headboard. The, what are the ones with the fingers? They're not as dense."

"Figures," I said.

"Wisps of smoke on your shoulders."

"Whispers."

"Can they go yet?"

"No," I said, frustrated because they were refusing.

"Okay, new tactic. What made them come out?"

He was talking about them the way I talk about them, as separate from me, even though they're both part of and not part of me. I don't know if he realized he was doing it.

But he was still waiting for my answer. "Nightmare," I said, and they furled and unfurled against me, stirring up the sheets and blankets as they flowed down my arms, along my legs and back up.

"Do they come out like that every time you have a nightmare?"

"Not quite so . . . disturbed," I said. Usually when I woke up from a nightmare, they were there, at my back, calm and quiet. Waiting and patient.

"Can you at least pull them back enough that I can get out the door and get Virgil?"

"Why Virgil?" Virgil meant more questions. "And why didn't you go for the door first?"

"I couldn't just leave you in here alone," he said, like it was a matter of fact.

I would've left me alone in here.

"I need to get Virgil," he was saying, and I sighed, the whispers sighing with me. "I can hear both of you do that," he said.

"You can hear them?"

"Yes," he said. "They were a lot louder a minute ago."

"Were they howling?" I asked him. Because they seemed to like that one more than shrieking or screaming, although they do that too.

"Yes. Worse than wolves. They do that one a lot?"

"Often enough," I said. We had meandered off the topic, and I was content to stay there. But Greg wasn't.

"Virgil," he said firmly. Or at least as firmly as he could when I could hear the tremor in his voice.

I nodded, closing my eyes. My heart had finally slowed. Could they go? We needed to answer Virgil's questions that my most recent nightmare would create, and that couldn't happen if they were hovering. Yes, they said, and they faded. The feel of their fingers lingered on my shoulders and neck.

Greg stepped cautiously away from the wall. When the unease in the air didn't return, he snagged his jeans off the floor and pulled them on before he went over to the door. "Wait here," he said. He left the door open and disappeared down the hallway, not toward the bedroom at the end, but back toward security and the kitchen.

I don't do waiting, so, I slid off the bed grabbing my clothes off the floor and hurriedly pulling them on, fully intending to follow him. He was back before I could make it more than a couple steps toward the door.

"Virgil wants to know where you would be more comfortable talking," he said.

"Here is fine," I said. He nodded and disappeared again; then I heard two sets of footsteps down the hall coming back toward me. The quiet padding of bare feet, and the tread of boots. Greg came in first, Virgil followed. Still fully dressed. Does he ever sleep? Or does he sleep in his clothes?

"You had another nightmare?" he asked me, his voice sharp.

"Yes," I said. Greg sat down on the bed next to me, his arm slipping around my waist. Virgil's eyes flicked down and back up. There was a moment where I thought he smiled, pleased with something, like a Cheshire cat, but it was there and gone, and I couldn't be sure it had ever been there to begin with.

"Tell me about it," Virgil said.

I balked because what was there to tell? It was a nightmare. But they were both waiting, steady and implacable, and if I didn't tell him, he would keep badgering me.

I didn't have to tell him where the house came from.

"I was in a house, and the walls started bleeding," I said. "It wasn't scary until the hands came out."

144

"You're okay with bleeding walls," Greg said, "but not hands?"

"Bleeding walls is cliché," I told him.

Virgil made a noise. "Could we stay on point please?"

"Sorry," I said, although I wasn't. "So, the hands came out, and those I backed up from, and then there was someone behind me, so I turned around."

"Who was behind you?" Virgil asked.

My heart sped up, which was stupid, because it was just a dream. I could feel Greg's fingers flex against me, his arm tightening against my back. "Red Eye," I told Virgil.

Virgil turned and went out the door. He paused, turned back, and looked at me. "Did he say anything to you?"

I didn't want to answer that. Virgil locked eyes with me. "I see," he said, and he turned away again.

"Does he always do that?" I asked Greg.

"No," he said. "Sometimes he explains it." He got up, loosening and pulling his arm back from my waist. "I'm going to go see what he's doing." He headed out of the room.

Well, I wasn't waiting around for them to report back to me, if they even do, so, I hopped off the bed and followed him.

Virgil had gone to his security room and was watching the monitors. Something moved; we could follow its path along the monitors as it circled the exterior of the fence, pacing steadily, moving with its head low. A prowl, and every so often, it raised its head, baring those white fangs at the cameras. I backed out of the room and set my back against the wall.

"Meg, breathe. Just breathe." Greg had followed me out of the room. His hands were on my face.

"As much as I hate to break this up, Meg, have you seen him after every nightmare you've had recently?" Virgil had come out as well.

145

I was trying to think it through and breathe at the same time.

"Now?" Greg said. "You're going to do this right now?"

"Yes," Virgil said. "This is time sensitive."

"Yes," I said finally.

"Causation," Virgil said, and he went striding down the hallway, without explaining what any of that meant.

Greg scooped me up.

"Hey!" I protested. "I can walk!"

"Do you want to walk?" he asked me.

Well, I guess I was already up there. "No."

"Okay then," he said, and he headed back to what was currently our room. He climbed into the bed without setting me down, then settled us against the pillows, one arm wrapped under my back, one hand splayed against my thigh. He kissed the top of my head, his nose in my hair. "Get some sleep. I've got you."

∞

When I woke up, he wasn't on the bed next to me. I got up and headed for the kitchen.

He was there, I was relieved to see. He smiled at me when I walked in and set the cup of coffee he had just poured down on the counter, nudging it toward me. I sat down and slid it the rest of the way toward me. He grabbed another mug and poured himself a new cup. Then he leaned back against the counter lining the wall, sipping his coffee and watching me.

"Ah, there you both are," Virgil said, striding in. "For your information, according to the security tapes, he gave up sometime around 4:00 in the morning." He poured himself a cup of coffee. "Oh, and Bolt is outside the gate asking to come in. I told her to fuck off."

Greg had come around the island to where I was seated, and at Virgil's words he choked on his coffee. "You what?" he coughed.

"I told her to fuck off. You told me the politicians finally managed to piss you off. And she's sleeping with one of them." He took a sip of his coffee. "Hence, she can fuck off."

Greg was still coughing. "I wasn't aware she was dating anyone."

"Not dating. Sleeping with. Some sort of friends with benefits arrangement."

"You ever going to tell me how you manage to get a hold of this type of information?"

"No."

Greg was silent for a moment. "You have information on me I'm not aware of?"

"Nothing I could blackmail you with," Virgil said. "You're squeaky clean and incredibly boring." He snapped his fingers. "Oh wait, there was the one thing, but your employers know about that don't they?" He was back to that mercurial mood.

"What thing?" I asked looking between the two of them. Because despite the way he was acting, Virgil had made me curious. What? Greg knows about my thing, he read my file. I don't have a file to read; Virgil is the closest I'm going to get unless Greg coughs it up.

Virgil saw the expression on Greg's face, and he changed targets. "High school bullshit. Certainly nothing as bad as what you did, huh, Meg?"

I paled but stared him defiantly in the face. "Then you know exactly what I could do to you if you piss me off," I said.

I could put up with his questions but not with that.

He chuckled and wagged a finger at me. "I knew there was a reason I liked you."

Right now, the feeling wasn't mutual. But apparently, he had accomplished his goal because I was distracted from whatever Greg had done and had also changed targets.

"Why are you friends with him?" I asked Greg.

"Gregor is not the type to throw away a useful ally. Even if I am an asshole. He puts up with a lot of shit he really shouldn't be putting up with." Well, I guess Virgil is nothing if not honest.

Greg watched him steadily. "You have your good points."

"Why, thank you. I didn't know you thought well of me."

"Don't push it," Greg said.

"Hmm. I suppose I shouldn't. And as far I can tell, Bolt is still at the gate yelling at the callbox. She might be fast, but even she can't get over that fence."

"Why not?" I asked. Surely someone with her speed could just run up it.

"It's electrified. The moment she touches it, well, it won't be pretty, let's put it that way."

"You sure do have a lot of protection against other heroes in place." Although those protections had been good for keeping Red Eye from getting into the compound itself, even if he could access the grounds.

"Most of them don't entirely trust me since I won't get in bed with the rest of them. I don't need some eager beaver heading off a potential threat just because we don't see eye to eye on how operations should work." He poured himself some more coffee. "So, what do you want me to do about her?"

"Does she know we're here?" Greg asked.

"I didn't tell her, but she seems to think this is where you would've gone to ground, so to say. Something about you going off the rails and disappearing with an asset?"

Greg clenched his jaw.

"I can take her out if you want me to," Virgil said, "but I wouldn't recommend it. It'll just attract more attention, and you certainly can't leave while she's here. I mean, you could, but she's not blind. You'd have to take to the air. No way you could outrun her in that thing you showed up in."

"Great," I said. "More people we have to wait out."

"I could try talking to her," Greg said.

"I would not recommend that course of action either," Virgil said, "because right now she just suspects you're here. Talk to her and she'll know. And you don't know that she won't be back with reinforcements."

Greg hesitated.

"You can't trust her, Gregor. She won't bite the hand that feeds her, and you know it. If you want to protect your *friend* here, you need to let Bolt pace herself out. Because she's here to retrieve her. Not to help you." But he sounded quite cheerful about the whole thing.

Greg rubbed his forehead. "Do you have a way to contain her?"

"What, so more people can come looking for her when she doesn't come home?" Virgil chuckled. "You are too used to just being able to punch through things that are in your way. Face it; you two are stuck here at least until she leaves." Greg made a noise, like he was going to protest, but Virgil kept going, his voice strident. "And I wouldn't recommend trying that anyway, with the way Red Eye was hanging around."

"Are you absolutely positive I can't talk sense into her?

149

We could use the help."

Virgil snorted. "You don't even know if that is the real Bolt. You know what Red Eye does."

"Patrice couldn't shift into other people." The expression on his face changed, like he had just let something he had meant to keep to himself slip.

"Are you aware of every power he's acquired? Because even I don't have that information, so I think you need to assume he has capabilities you don't know about." Virgil was continuing the conversation like he hadn't noticed anything was wrong. But I could feel the sudden tension that was in the air between them, and Virgil's eyes had flickered again.

"What do you mean every power he's acquired?" I asked.

Virgil crossed his arms, the tone of his voice lecturing, "You need to tell her. You're letting her stumble around in the dark in the name of protection."

"Tell me what?" I snapped. Because I was getting really tired of having to drag information out of people.

Greg was clenching his jaw. "Meg."

"Don't 'Meg' me!" I shouted at him. "Just fucking tell me!"

Greg looked like he was caught, his mouth working as he considered what he had to say to me. "He takes people's powers," he finally spat out. "He tortures them, he kills them, and somehow he's absorbing their powers. And then he uses those powers to do it again."

"Oh," I said.

"And now he wants yours. And I think we can all agree that would be very, very bad."

Well, duh.

"There," said Virgil. "She's all caught up now, and you got that off your chest. I am going to see if our uninvited guest has left yet." He left the kitchen, which left Greg and me alone together.

The silence was heavy.

"Meg—" he started to say.

"Don't," I said. "Don't try to defend yourself. You should have told me the truth from the start. If you couldn't have trusted anything else about me, you could've at least trusted my own self-interest in not fucking dying. And maybe, just maybe I wouldn't have fought and argued with you about everything you tried to convince me to do!"

And now it was my turn to be the one ranting because I had had enough of the pushing and prodding, the secrets, the drips of information, of being forced in a direction I didn't want to go. Of being treated like a chess piece.

"But no! You had to keep treating me like a pawn that you could just shove in the right direction and win the game! I'm not Patrice! I don't need rescuing from myself and saving me isn't going to fix you!" I was shouting again, and the whispers and figures were at my back, pulling at my arms. Swirling and curling around my legs, shadows stretched out along the floor rising up and looming by my side. And Greg was backing away from me, pressed against the wall.

God help me, in that moment I liked seeing the fear in his eyes.

Maybe I was meant to be a villain.

I turned and left the kitchen and headed for the stairs. I was done, I was leaving. I didn't care if Bolt was still outside; I would make her tear herself to pieces.

Greg was calling me. "Meg! Don't, please! It wasn't like that!" I ignored him. He couldn't follow me past the kitchen door, so thick was the fear swirling around me. The rage over the loss of control of my life, of being pushed and pulled, my choices taken from me one by one because I was expected to just let other people decide what was best for me, was so strong their range seemed to have doubled. More than unease, I could almost taste the terror in the air.

We flowed forward, through the living room, up the steps, and at the top of the stairs, I tried to spin the lock, and found it was stuck. I turned. Virgil was at the bottom of the stairs, one hand palm out at me. He was sweating and looked like he was fighting not to turn and run.

"Let me out." The whispers repeated me, *out, out, out.*

"No," he said.

"Let. Me. Out," I growled, and the whispers howled, and the figures and shadows rushed him. Then Virgil was screaming and backing away and falling and I let him go. He lay still at the bottom of the stairs. I turned away and unlocked the door.

I strode across the empty space between the door back down and the front door and unlocked that one too. And then I was outside in the sun. And I had to consider the fact that I hadn't thought about the fence and gate or the power-stealing demon creature waiting for me.

But I walked down the long drive anyway, ignoring the figure on the roof behind me. Had Virgil been wrong about him leaving, or had he come back undetected while we were in the kitchen? In the end, it made no difference. Let him come for me and find out just what kind of target I was.

And he did.

He dove at me, with the flapping of leathery wings and snatched me up by the shoulders. The whispers and I screamed, sound and fury and fear, and it swirled into the air with us and hit him. With a screaming shriek of his own he crashed us into the ground on the other side of the fence. He recovered before I did, still trying to pick myself back up out of the undergrowth when he tackled me. I hammered the fear into him again, but this time he laughed and turned it back on me. The whispers and figures fled. And so did the sun.

CHAPTER TEN

When I woke up, I couldn't move.

Well, not precisely. I tried, yanking at my wrists and ankles, but they were shackled to whatever surface I was resting on. I lifted my head as much as I could, stuck spread-eagle, and looked around.

Peeling paint, water stains on the ceiling and walls, cabinets with sinks, their doors askew. They looked empty as far as I could tell. What I could see of the floor looked like vinyl tile, the pieces cracked and scraped, parts of them missing. The room looked like it belonged to a derelict hospital in a horror movie. Of fucking course it would. Where else would a melodramatic power stealing demon creature bring me?

I lay my head back down, straining my ears. All I heard was silence. As far as I could tell, there was no one else in the room with me.

That didn't bring any sense of relief. If he wasn't in a hurry to kill me, that meant he knew he had plenty of time.

Oh God, Greg. I flashed back to his face. Had I really done that to him? How could I have used the fear on him like that? A sob caught in my throat, and I closed my eyes, clenching my jaw. Not the time, Meg.

I wouldn't blame him if he wasn't coming to my rescue.

There was the sound of a cart being wheeled down a hallway. It was coming toward me. I began yanking at the restraints again, trying to squirm away from the door, which opened with a bang.

"So, you're finally awake, little lady," he said, looming into my view.

I spat in his face.

He backhanded me. I could taste blood in my mouth when the impact made me bite my cheek.

"Behave," he snarled at me.

"Or what?" I spat back. I knew what he wanted, and I was going to fight him every step of the way.

He punched me in the collarbone.

I felt it snap.

I screamed and bucked, tearing at the restraints, fighting against the whispers who howled at me to let them out because I knew he would just turn them back on me, and I needed to hold onto their power for as long as I could against him. Any control I kept was control he didn't have yet. He waited until I gave up, breathing in ragged pants.

"If I can do that to you bare handed, just wait until you find out what I can do with a knife," he told me.

I might have whimpered. The whispers were screaming their rage in my ears.

He laughed. "Let's get started, shall we?"

He touched my face.

∞

I was back in the house, facing the front door. The only

sound was that of a ticking clock.

I didn't remember there being that kind of clock in the house. I would know. I revisit it in my dreams often enough. Slowly I turned to face the rest of the room.

The front door also didn't lead straight into the living room where the largest group of people had been.

And there definitely wasn't a yawning, black maw in the floor of the real house. Now that I was facing it, I could hear the whispers coming from it, and in it, something moved.

To my left, something else moved, and I turned to face it.

His red eyes stared at me. "How interesting." His voice sounded like it was coming from the bottom of a well. "Normally, they can't follow me in here. I tell them not to, and then they can't."

"I never was very good at following orders," I said.

"How irritating of you."

I shrugged.

He looked away from me, at the house around us. "Ah, your dreams," he said. "I've been watching you since I first tasted your nightmares in the air. So much guilt. So much fear. How strange that the shape of it is here."

"Are you done monologuing?" I asked.

He waved a hand at me. "Go away now."

I could feel something tearing, and far away I could hear my own voice screaming. My body here, wherever here was, started to disintegrate, pieces floating away like confetti.

"*No*," the whispers and I said. My body rushed back together.

His eyes narrowed as he watched me. "Fine. Then I suppose I can let you watch me. I've always wondered what it does to them when I take the essence."

He stepped onto the edge of the maw. He sighed and shuddered, shutting those red, red eyes. "I've known power like this before."

I could see the blackness traveling up his leg, and as it moved, I could feel it pulling away from me. It hurt, like someone was trying to tear my chest open, and something living fluttered inside, trying to flee. I staggered and fell to my knees. I pulled back, resisting, and the pain of it made me want to scream. I couldn't let him have them. They were mine and I was theirs. Snarling at me, he pulled harder.

The maw was getting smaller, the pain greater, traveling up my neck and head, down my legs, as he and I struggled for control over the darkness. There was torment in it, and fury. And despite my resistance, I was losing, the power leaking away from me, every beat of my heart weaker, slower. In my ears, I could hear the whispers calling for me.

So I reached for them, my fingers brushing the edge closest to me.

They were angry.

They reached back for me, and my hand slammed down, into the maw. I could hear the howling, the rushing of the figures, beating in time with my heart.

He opened his eyes, rage in his face. "NO!" he shrieked. "They're dead, those gods are dead!"

No, we're not, the whispers said. Because they remembered what they forgot.

He screamed and rushed at me. I knew I couldn't let him touch me here, in the house, so I rolled away, into the maw.

I was falling into its darkness, and the figures caught me. They swirled around me while the whispers laughed, and the shadows stretched. I was theirs and they were mine. Anchor in more than name.

157

Vengeance, they whispered.

∞

Someone slapped me. I tried to strike back, but they caught my hand. For a moment I stared at it, uncomprehending. When had the restraints come off?

"Good, you're awake," Bolt said. "Get up, Fuck-up."

"What—" my tongue felt thick in my mouth, my whole body ached, and I wasn't sure I could get up.

With a disgusted sigh, she pulled me up, and I screamed when it pulled on my broken collarbone. She slapped a hand over my mouth. "Would you shut up? Greg and Virgil have him distracted, and if you're over here losing your fucking mind, Greg's going to lose focus." She helped me slide off the table, supporting me on the unbroken side. "God damn, you're a fucking mess. No, don't look! I don't need you passing out on me!" Despite her support I staggered. She yanked me back up and I bit back a yelp.

"Good girl," she said. "I've got you, come on. We'll go slow. I wouldn't want to try carrying you at full tilt in this condition anyway. I don't know what's damaged."

"How did you-" I gasped as we headed out into the hallway. I wasn't sure how I managed to walk at all. Adrenaline must be one hell of a drug. She was practically dragging me down the hall, hurrying me past sagging doorways, fallen ceiling tiles. God this place was nasty looking. "How did you find me?"

"Dumbass didn't think to check for a tail. I saw him snatch you up, so I followed him here. And not being stupid, like some people, I got other heroes for back up."

I wasn't sure if it was a dig at me for leaving Virgil's safe house or at Greg for leaving her standing at the callbox.

We were at a set of stairs, and she was trying to hustle me down them, but one of my knees didn't quite want to bend. She tsked, looking at it. "Hold on, this is going to hurt." She popped something as she twisted my knee, and I howled. Then she had me pinned against the wall of the stairwell, her hand over my mouth again. "Get it together," she snapped. "Can you bend your knee now?" I tried, and it bent, although it hurt like a bitch, so I nodded as best I could with her hand still pinned to my face. "Good," she said. "Keep moving."

She practically pulled me down the rest of the stairs.

In the distance, I could hear crashing. She was shoving me down another long hallway, yanking me to the right and out what used to be a set of double doors. I could see what was left of them in the weed-choked yard in front of us. There was a Hummer sitting on what used to be a driveway or parking lot. A real one, not the shitty ones you get from the dealership nowadays. Grade A military, an actual Humvee. But I'm just gonna call it a Hummer because that's what I'll remember it as.

"I'm gonna drop you off in Virgil's car. You will fucking stay put while I tag him out. Because he is going to get you out of here."

"Why Virgil?" I gasped as she pulled me toward the Hummer.

"Because it's his fucking car, and he's not going to let me drive it."

She pulled a door open and shoved me in. I yelped, and as she shut the door practically on my foot, she said, "Suck it up. Don't fucking move."

She disappeared.

It felt like a frighteningly long time before the driver side door popped open and Virgil hauled himself in. The door shut itself, and I heard the engine growl to life. "You buckled-?" Virgil started as he looked back at me. "Nope not gonna happen. Try not to fall off the seat."

He hit the gas, and there was the clatter of gravel kicked up by the tires as the Hummer roared forward. I went ahead and fell onto the floor in front of the seat. The box-like space would keep me better contained anyway. There was no way I was staying up in anything with the way he was driving. And now I was slamming into the door and the hump-like metal of what would be the center aisle in a regular car whenever he took a turn.

"Damn it," he said and reached a hand back, palm facing me. I stopped, pinned against the door. The Hummer bounced, and I stayed stuck to the door instead of bouncing into the air with it.

I was staring out the window, watching the tree branches flash by. I couldn't move my head to look anywhere else, which was the only reason I saw when we roared through the gate onto Virgil's compound. The Hummer tilted forward, and then I could hear the sound of the engine echoing off the walls of a tunnel. The movement stopped, then silence except for the ticking of the engine as it cooled. The door next to me opened, and someone was pulling me out.

"Come on. Greg will rip my arms off if I don't get you patched up." Every jouncing movement made me breathe in hissing pants.

"You said Greg." I focused on the only thing that didn't cause physical pain.

"I like to poke the bear. I don't know why he still comes around. Probably the only friend I've got. The rest of them wrote me off a long time ago."

He was setting me down on a soft, cool surface. "Go to

sleep, Meg," he said. "You don't really want to be awake while I get you fixed." I felt something prick my arm and then was awash in warmth. A different whisper in my ears, calm, serene but with an order all the same. "Sleep," it said, and even if I wanted to fight it, I couldn't. I closed my eyes.

∞

I was in a new dream, a place I remembered but had forgotten. The faint scent of the sea lingered in the air, yet I was surrounded by olive trees, a grove that slowly became clearer. Greens and browns, gnarled branches, heavy with their fruit. Grass beneath my feet, I could feel it pricking my soles. Where are my shoes?

I lifted my skirt, heavy against my legs, the fabric soft and supple under my hands. My feet were definitely bare. But what was I wearing? There was so much of this tunic-like dress, and for a moment I was distracted by the weave of it.

The whispers curled against my shoulders. Their sighs in my ears captured my attention and pulled it from whatever I was dressed in. *Home*, they said. I could see the blue of the ocean through the trees now. Home where? I asked them, but it slipped away again.

I could feel the brush of their fingers and my curls tickling my neck, but when I reached a hand up to move my hair, I found it was already up. The figures were swirling away from me, furling around the trees and beckoning me onward. The shadows stretched away, and my feet followed their path.

We were moving forward, through the olive grove, down the steep hill they were rooted on. And then there was cool sand beneath my feet, between one breath and the next, but I didn't remember reaching the bottom of that grove. There was the heady smell of salt in the wind.

Sand and surf and the olive grove. There had been power here, if only we could remember what it was.

As peaceful as it was, something lurked under the surface, and something loomed in the air. A power more than what we were was awakening.

Red Eye had been wrong. They had never died, only faded. They were imprisoned or sleeping, somewhere we couldn't reach at this moment. Because we had left it or never gone?

In this place, I could choose. Remember, or forget? The remembering would be a long time coming, and in the meantime we might forget again. But it would come.

If we remembered, we would have vengeance for what he tried to do to us. I was theirs and they were mine, and we would not be parted by someone as insignificant as he was. It was an insult that he had done as well as he had against us.

All of this and more the whispers told me. Before I could wake, I would have to choose. But sleeping was also a choice. I could stay in this place with them. For a little while at least. But someone was waiting for me.

The whispers could hear them, on the wind, like an out-of-tune radio. Voices drifting in the air. And I knew them, the timbres echoing around me.

"Meg, wake up. You have to wake up." Serene, and calm, but an order all the same. But I didn't have to. I could choose not to. And I've never done well with commands.

It was the other voice that did it. "Meg—" was all it said at first. "Meg, please wake up."

Choose, said the whispers. Home will always be here. The remembering and forgetting won't be.

Why not? I asked them.

162

Sleep long enough, and we will die. Or you will die, and we will lose you, they told me. It made no difference which; the answer would be the same to them.

Which made sleeping a different kind of choice altogether.

We went down the beach a little further while I thought. And then I chose. We would remember, but in the meantime we would forget.

∞

When I woke up, I was in a hospital bed. Somewhere I registered the scene wasn't right for a hospital, but it was what was on the other side of the room from me that caught my attention. Greg was huddled in a chair across the room, head in hands. He looked up; I assume because he had heard the change in my breathing. He surged up from the chair and staggered across the empty space between us.

"Oh God, Meg." His hands were on my face, and he was resting his forehead against mine. "I thought I was going to lose you."

"I'm sorry," I croaked. My voice felt rusty, hoarse, like it hadn't just been damaged from screaming, but had lain unused and collecting dust.

He was brushing a thumb back and forth across my cheek. "It's okay," he said. "I'm sorry, too. I should have told you. I—" he stopped and kissed me, lips soft on mine. "Just, don't do that again. Please."

"Which part?" I had to ask because I was ashamed of what I had done to him, and I tried to move my face away because I didn't deserve his affection after that. But his hand was in the way of my chin and I couldn't look away from him.

All I could do was drop my eyes from his, and I couldn't keep them there, they kept drifting back up to his.

"Don't put yourself in danger like that! You could've died! He - Jesus, Meg. What did you think I meant?"

Tears were pricking my eyes. Still, he wouldn't move his hands away from my face. I didn't know how to answer him.

He stayed there, steadily staring into my eyes, and he looked frightened.

"I scared you," I finally said. It was as close to an admission of guilt as I could stand in the moment.

"Yes, you fucking scared me! You—" he paused, moving his hands away. "Did you do that to me on purpose?"

I looked down, and for once didn't defend myself. I hadn't sent the whispers after him, but I didn't pull them back either. It made me as guilty as if I had.

He got up and moved away from me. "God damn it, Meg." His back was to me, hands in his hair.

There was a long silence.

I couldn't stand it any longer. "I'm sorry. I didn't mean-" I stopped mid-sentence. I wasn't sure how much of it had been intentional, but it didn't matter because I had done it. I had chosen not to stop once I realized what I was doing.

He turned to face me. "You're sorry! You—" he stopped and I flinched at the wounded look on his face.

There was another long silence, and this time I was afraid to break it because I was afraid if I said the wrong thing, he would walk out the door. My heart in my throat, I waited. I knew he could hear how rapidly it was beating.

Finally, he sighed and sat back down on the edge of the hospital bed. "Meg, calm down."

"Does telling people to calm down ever work on them?" I asked weakly.

"No," he said, regarding me seriously. "Don't you ever, ever do that to me again."

"I won't," I promised, shame making my face burn.

"Good," he said.

Again, with the silence. Thick and heavy it filled the room. When I tried to swipe my usable arm across my face, I felt something pull against the skin. There was an IV attached to me. For a moment I was distracted by the realization that Virgil really is always prepared, but Greg's presence was so still next to me. I hadn't realized I had gotten used to his usual coiled energy. It pulled me back to the tension of the moment.

"Are you…" and I hesitated, but had to ask, "are you still mad at me?"

"Yes," he said.

There wasn't much I could say to that. I hadn't really expected a different answer, so I fiddled with the blankets. He set his hands on top of mine. "I will get over it," he said.

"Okay," I said. I tried to keep the relief out of my voice, but from the look he gave me, I knew he heard it.

"I would ask you to come here," he said, "but Virgil won't tell me how much of you he had to fix, so I don't know if you should be moving."

"I feel okay," I lied. I felt like shit. He shot me another look, but he didn't call me on it.

"I told him not to give you morphine. I wasn't sure if it would be safe for you in your condition."

"I would've been fine," I said. Well, eventually I would've been fine. Anything that affects my cognitive thinking seems to do a number on my system. Like going into shock, but not. And I've never asked if that's typical or something unique to me because of my power. "Virgil—" I paused. "Well, I'm not sure if the whispers would've known that he was

165

helping."

"They talk to you?"

"Yes?" I said cautiously.

"As in independent thought talking to you?"

"Yes," I said. "Where are you going with this?"

"I've never heard of anyone's power working like that."

I shrugged. And then hissed when it pulled on my collarbone.

Greg's jaw tightened, and his hands were on my face again, I think because he wasn't sure where else he could touch me without hurting me. He made a frustrated sound. "I don't like this."

"I told you that you wouldn't," Virgil said from the doorway.

"It's just a broken bone," I said. Greg was grinding his teeth again. "Stop it," I said grumpily.

"It was not just a broken bone," Virgil said coming into the room. "Move," he told Greg. Greg glared at him but moved off the bed, and Virgil took his place, his hands hovering over me, brow furrowed. "Everything seems to still be in place." He moved away, and Greg practically shouldered him aside to get back next to me.

"I thought you were telekinetic," I said.

"I am. But to be able to use it for moving finer or delicate things, you need to know how they work. You think I could unlock a door without knowing how the tumblers work? Sometimes it's more complicated than just flicking aside the deadbolt. You have to be able to, hmm, sense how it's all put together?"

That sounded more useful than just being able to throw things around without using your hands.

But I had other questions, and the vague sense that not

everything was as it seems.

"How long was I out for?" I asked. Virgil's eyes flickered, and Greg looked down. "What?" I demanded. "How long?"

"About four weeks," Virgil said, as if he wasn't sure. He had turned and was rummaging in a cabinet before he came back over to the bed.

Greg shot him a look, and I got the feeling that Virgil knew exactly how long I had been unconscious, but he didn't say anything. And I wasn't sure what to do with that information anyway.

"As it is, I think you can move her to a more comfortable room, and then we will need to discuss our next move," Virgil said, as he reached around Greg, pressing a piece of gauze over where the IV met my skin. With his other hand he gave the IV a gentle tug and pulled it free. "Hold that there for a minute," he said. Before I could move my hand, Greg had placed his fingers over the gauze.

But I had something more important that I needed to concentrate on.

"Next move?" I asked, looking back and forth at their faces. "Is he—" I swallowed. "Is he still out there?"

"Yes," Greg growled. "If Bolt hadn't—"

"Bolt," Virgil said, his tone firm, "was being rational in exercising caution."

"We should have pressed our advantage! I had—"

"You had nothing! He was smoke!"

"She could've contained him—" Greg had turned, letting go of my arm, his hands on the edge of the bed as he argued with Virgil.

"Yes, and what would've happened if he got into her lungs in that form?"

I could hear the metal of the bed groaning.

"I will make you pay to repair that. You can't find beds made like this anymore," Virgil said.

"Maybe you should take some anger management classes," I said to Greg. He shot me a look but let go of the bed. From the number of irritated looks he was giving us, he was going to run out of his quota for the year. He stood up, arms crossed, staring at Virgil.

Virgil sighed but turned his back on us. I looked at the two of them, confused. That was until Greg flipped back the blankets and I realized the only thing that was separating us was one of those thin, paper hospital gowns. I went bright red and made a grab for the blankets again and yelped when the movement pulled on what felt like everything. Greg sighed.

"Don't you sigh at me!" I snapped, angry because everything hurt, and I did not want to be exposed to anyone. I didn't care that one of them had definitely seen me naked, and I didn't even want to know if Virgil had. There's a different kind of vulnerability when you're hurt and in pain, and nobody wants to be in a paper gown in front of anyone.

I mean, unless that's what you're into. I won't judge, but I don't want to know about it.

"Then stop running headlong into danger," Greg said, pulling the blankets back over me before he scooped me and them up. He marched me out of the room. I saw the sign on the door as he turned down the hallway.

"He put me in the lab?!"

"You know he was just messing with you about that, right?"

"No," I groused, glaring at Virgil, who was following us down the hall.

Greg brought me back to his room and settled me in a

chair while he moved the blankets on the bed out of the way; then he piled pillows against the headboard. He had started back across to me when Virgil spoke up.

"You need to let her try walking."

Greg glared at him.

"The two of you can glare at me all you want. She needs to try walking."

I clutched at the blankets because I was not going to be able to drag them across the floor with me to stay covered. Greg ignored him and gently hoisted me up and put me on the bed so that I was resting against the pillows, then tucked the rest of the blankets around me. "I'm not making her do anything right now," he said, sitting next to me.

"What happened to my clothes?"

"They weren't salvageable," Virgil said.

And all the rest of my stuff was back at Greg's apartment because he had rushed us out of there without anything.

"Rest," Greg said. "I'll see what I can do about clothes for you." He stood up.

"Don't," I said.

"Don't what?" he asked me. "Find you clothes?"

"Don't go," I said.

"Well, I'm going to go," Virgil said, and he shut the door behind him.

"Okay," Greg said as he sat back down, with one hand on my face, he kissed me.

CHAPTER ELEVEN

Bolt ended up going through Virgil's storage and brought me clothes she found in there. "I don't know how well these will fit," she told me, "since I'm going off approximation, but I figured you might feel less vulnerable this way." She tossed the clothes - which included a Kevlar vest - down onto the bed.

I stared at it.

"Greg told me you don't want to get shot," she said by way of explanation.

"Thanks," I said.

"Uh huh. Don't get cocky, you could still fuck up."

"I'll do my best to avoid that."

"Finally," she said and smiled at me.

It took me a long time to get dressed. I was sweating and felt nauseated by the time I was done getting clothes on. I didn't even want to consider socks and shoes. I wasn't actually sure what had happened to mine or where they were, and Bolt hadn't brought me new ones. But I guess going barefoot wasn't the worst.

Don't let someone break your collarbone. The recovery

sucks.

Greg had tried to hover outside the door, but Virgil had managed to convince him to leave me alone on some pretense or another. I wasn't sure what it was; I hadn't been listening because I was trying to work up the courage to get my arm through the shirt.

There was a knock on the door. "Can I come in?" Greg asked.

"Yes," I said from the floor. Once I had gotten the pants on, I had just sat down where I was, rather than trying to climb back into the bed. It had seemed like the easier option. I wasn't sure what Virgil had done to help prevent atrophy, but my muscles seemed to work fine. I stayed on the floor because it just felt like too much effort to get up. The one time I said anything to Virgil about it, his response was that it wasn't unexpected.

Of course I had asked him about it because he had absolutely come back before Bolt had even brought me any clothes and made me try walking. Meanwhile, Greg tried to mother hen me and wasted time arguing with Virgil about it in the first place. Eventually I had ignored them both and gotten out of the damn bed on my own. I think I made it about five steps before my knee hurt too much to keep going.

Huh, Virgil must have my number because that was probably the best way to get me over being embarrassed about the paper gown.

Greg opened the door and took in the scene. "Meg," he said.

"You say my name an awful lot," I said.

He huffed. "You should be resting."

"I am resting."

He joined me on the floor. "How're you feeling?"

"Better," I said. It wasn't entirely a lie.

Very carefully, he laid an arm across my shoulders and pulled me into him. "Hmm," he said.

Virgil knocked on the doorframe. "You two need to come down the living room. I've got something to show you."

Greg moved his arm so it was wrapped around my waist and lifted me up as he stood. "Can you walk that far?" he asked me.

"I'm fine," I insisted.

I was pretty sure he thought I wouldn't notice just how much of my weight he was taking as he helped me down the hallway. "I know what you're doing," I told him.

"I'm not doing anything."

I snorted.

"Set her down, Greg. She's not stupid," Bolt said from by the bookcases. She was perusing the shelves while Virgil started messing with his TV. "Jesus, Virg, how much porn for housewives do you need?"

"Romance," Virgil grunted from behind the TV, "is an underrated genre." He stepped away from it. "There, hooked up."

"Couldn't you have done that without the dramatics?" Bolt asked, still running a hand along the book spines.

"Sometimes you need the hands-on method," he said, flicking his hand at the TV, which turned on. There was static. He waved at us. "Sit. She shouldn't be on that knee for too long."

"I'm not on the knee," I said. Greg cleared his throat.

Virgil gave him a long look. Greg set me down and kept pace with me as I hobbled my way to the couch. When I paused, he set his hands on my waist. "Greg," I growled at him. "I can sit down on my own." After a moment of hesitation, he let go of me, and I sank slowly onto the couch. He settled next to me, our thighs touching, his arm slung across the back of the couch behind me.

"What are we doing?" I asked. "Is it movie night? Because I'm gonna need popcorn." Greg chuckled, and the sound made me feel warm.

"No," Virgil said. "We are going to review the footage I shot from our most recent engagement."

"You recorded that?" Greg asked.

"I record all my encounters."

Bolt snorted. "Are you that narcissistic that you have to watch yourself fight?"

Virgil gazed at her steadily. "It's a first-person view since the camera is on me. I don't feature at all. What I want to see is what the enemy did."

She flopped down onto the couch next to me. "Why?"

"Why do football coaches watch rushes of the other team's plays?" Virgil asked and then answered his own question. "To prepare."

He started the tape with a flick of his hand.

I watched as they rushed the hospital doors and Virgil pulled them off, flinging them back over Greg's head before he had even reached them. I had assumed Greg had thrown them that far. I probably should have realized they would've been smashed in if Greg had been the one who hit them. Virgil waved again, and the tape sped forward, then back to playing at regular speed. He had jumped it ahead to where it looked like they were in what was left of the hospital cafeteria, and Red Eye was there, still in human shape. He was dodging Greg's swings, sliding just out of his reach, and when Virgil yanked a table at him from across the room, it was like he caught it in the air before it changed course and flung itself at Virgil. Virgil bounced it up over himself.

"There," Virgil had paused it.

"There what?" Greg asked.

"Right there," Virgil said. "Watch again." The scene rewound and then repeated.

"All I see is you idiots not landing any hits," Bolt said. "Were you two even trying?"

"Not really," Greg scrubbed at his face. "Virgil said to avoid direct contact."

"That doesn't look like avoiding direct contact from Virgil," Bolt said.

"I was testing a theory," Virgil said, "and I got results."

"What results?" Greg said, sounding frustrated.

"It's in the small details," Virgil said, playing the scene again. He paused it, the table mid-flip.

"You got control back," I said.

Virgil clapped his hands and pointed at me. "Exactly. That table should've hit me if he still had control over turning my power back on me. You did something when he tried to take yours, Meg." He crouched down in front of me. "You need to tell me exactly what happened."

In case you haven't figured this out about me, I do not like talking about traumatic events, so I absolutely did not want to tell Virgil what happened in that hospital. Except Greg spoke up first.

"No," he said.

I think it was the first time I saw anger flit across Virgil's face. "We need to know if he has a weakness we can exploit."

"You are not making her relive that." Greg stood up, towering over Virgil.

Virgil rose slowly, and while he was shorter than Greg, his voice was strident and commanding, his presence more than the space he took up. "You cannot wrap her in cotton. She is not made of glass, and she is our only chance at figuring out how to take him down."

"Maybe," Bolt suggested, "you should let her answer for herself."

They all stopped and looked at me.

Being stared at by three heroes is not a comfortable experience.

But now I was mad because Greg had tried to answer for me, and you should know by now that I have a tendency to do the opposite of what people tell me to do, no matter if they're coming from a place of good intentions. I raised my chin. "Okay," I said.

"Meg—" Greg started, but I switched my gaze to his face, and he stopped.

"Lab. Let's go," Virgil said, holding out a hand to me. I took it, and he pulled me up. "You'll excuse me if I help your knee a bit." I nodded and started to follow him. Greg got up from the couch.

"No," I said.

"But—"

"No, Greg." It hurt to refuse him, but it would hurt more for him to know what took place in that room. "You don't want to hear this."

We left him standing by the couch.

∞

Virgil settled me on a stool and pulled one up in front of me where he sat, feet hooked into the rungs, and then made me start at the point where I had left him lying at the bottom of the stairs.

"From the top," he said.

"What's the top?" I asked, confused.

"From the moment you left my compound."

I swallowed, "I went outside, and he was waiting," I stopped, the experience of it too recent, and Virgil looked me in the eye.

"Meg," he said, "breathe. Don't feel it; just tell it." The command floated in the air, and I followed it, taking a breath. "Now, Red Eye, he was waiting?"

I started again, but now the encounter was distant, detached, as if I had only heard about it instead of living it. "He was on the roof. He had wings, and he grabbed me. The first time I hit him with the fear it worked, but the second time, he turned it back on me."

"What happened? Were you conscious? Did you see where he was taking you?"

"No, I think I fainted."

"When you woke up, where were you?"

"A room," I said, pausing as the image surged forward. I could remember the smell of mold and mildew, the scent of old blood.

"What kind of room?"

"You were in the building, you know what kind of room it—"

"Describe it anyway," he said, interrupting me.

"A hospital room. Cabinets, sinks, broken vinyl tiles."

"Where in the room were you?"

"What?" I asked, confused.

"Were you on the floor? Free to roam around?"

"On a table." I closed my eyes because I could hear the hollow ringing thud when I had kicked against it. "Metal. Restrained."

"What with?"

I had to think. The restraints had been hard and smooth, but not the biting edge of handcuffs. The sound they made when I had pulled against them had been a snapping, straining noise, not clinking. "Leather?" I said, half questioning.

"What could you hear?"

"Nothing, until," I had to pause to take a breath again, "until I could hear a cart coming down the hall."

"Is that when he came into the room?"

"Yes."

"Start again."

"What?"

"Start again; we're going to go over this bit by bit. What do you remember hearing?"

"When?"

"When he grabbed you. There should have been birds, insects. The area around the compound is full of wildlife."

I opened my mouth, closed it, and thought. The only sound I had heard had been the whispers howling in my ears. "Nothing," I said.

He made me go back through the description of the room I had woken up in, repeating questions I had already answered. What was I restrained to? With what?

"Next section," he said. "Did Red Eye say anything to you?"

"He called me little lady."

"Word for word, what did he say?"

He made me repeat it until he was satisfied that I was telling him exactly what our exchange had been.

"Is this the first time he called you little lady?"

"No," I said, and because I couldn't remember if I had told Virgil the other times, "he did it at the coffee shop and internet cafe too."

"You said you spat in his face?"

"Yes."

Virgil was silent for a moment, watching me. "Was that when he broke your collarbone?"

"Pretty much."

Virgil sighed. "Again, word for word, action for action."

He didn't have to make me repeat it as many times. I catch on quickly when I want to be done with something.

"What about the cart? Did you see it? What was it made of? What was on it?"

"No, but metal, I could hear the way the wheel was squeaking, and it rattled when he pushed it over the threshold."

"Next section, when he said he was going to get started, what happened?"

"He touched my face," but here my stomach revolted, and Virgil was shoving a trash can in my hands. I closed my eyes because at that moment I wanted Greg here, with his hand warm on my back. I pushed it away because I needed to finish. "I wasn't in the hospital anymore."

"Where were you?"

"In a house."

"Just a house?"

I didn't say anything, huddling over the trash can.

"I see," Virgil said, although I couldn't see how when I hadn't answered. "Tell me about the house. What was in it?"

"A clock, I could hear it ticking, a maw with – my power was in it," I thought about it, "a front door, but no furniture, no stairs, just the living room, and Red Eye."

"Is it the same house from the party?" he asked, and I looked at him, confused and wary, because I had been avoiding telling him anything about that house. At least, I thought I had been. Had I told him about the party? He had asked me so many questions, relentlessly pushing for answers. Had I slipped and given him information I meant to keep to myself?

"Greg shared a few details of your past with me," he said, and it came so smoothly that I wasn't sure why I suspected anything to start with. "Now, the house. Tell me about it. What were the colors? Were they the right colors? Was the front door the right door? Did you see the clock you could hear ticking? Did it sound familiar? Could you identify it as anything more than a clock?" His questions were so rapid-fire that I could only listen, intently trying to process them.

I had to pause and think again. "The only things with color were his eyes and the maw. Everything else was blank, it just feels blank."

"What color was the maw?"

"Black."

"Are you sure it was your power in it?"

"Yes."

"How did you know?"

"They were calling me."

Virgil was leaning forward, elbows on his knees, fingers steepled, the tips of his index fingers resting against his mouth. With the way he was sitting, I could only assume the reason his stool didn't tip over was because he was using his telekinesis to stay balanced.

"Was it only your power in it?" he asked.

"Yes."

"Back to the clock. What did it sound like?"

"A heartbeat," I said, the words coming out unbidden, because I hadn't stopped to consider the question before I answered.

"Whose?"

"I don't know."

"Did Red Eye say anything to you?"

"Yes, he said – that normally his victims can't follow him where he took me, and he was, surprised by the shape of it, like it's not usually a house?"

Virgil's feet came off the rungs of the stool, his weight shifting, his eyes narrowing. "What else did he say?"

"He told me to go away."

"What happened then?"

"I could," and I had to swallow as my stomach rolled again, "I could hear myself screaming, and something – I could feel it when my knee tore away."

"Dislocated," Virgil said soothingly, "otherwise Bolt wouldn't have been able to get it back into place to get you down the stairs."

"Okay," I said agreeably, strangely calm again.

"What happened next?"

"We refused," I said, "and stayed there in the house."

"He couldn't make you leave?"

"No."

Virgil's hands had changed position, his left arm crossed over his chest, the right elbow resting against it, hand up at his chin. "Who is we?"

"The whispers, figures, shadows and I."

"Can you still reach them?"

I sighed and called to them, and they were at my back, the whispers murmuring in my ears, the figures' fingers brushing my face, shadows pooled at the bottom of the stool, dripping off my feet.

Virgil made a startled noise, coming up off his stool for a brief moment before he cleared his throat and settled back on it, but not quickly enough for me to miss the tremor in his hands.

"It would appear that more than answers my question. Can you let them go, please?"

No, the whispers said. I could feel their reluctance, their need to stay by me. "No," I said, echoing them, "they want to stay."

Virgil stood up, his stool sliding across the room away from him, and he followed it. He settled back on it, facing me, just out of the range of the whispers and their compulsion.

None of his stools have wheels. It was such a small, every day, casual use of his telekinesis that for a moment I was jealous of the heroes who can go about their daily lives with no concern over how their power affects others.

He leaned forward again; eyes focused on mine. I think he was trying not to watch the way the figures' fingers would curl around me.

"Tell me what he said next," he said.

"That I could watch him take the essence."

"Do you know what he meant by that?"

"No."

"What did he do next?"

"He stepped onto the edge of the maw and started – pulling them into him. It hurt, they," and here I had to pause because the whispers were murmuring words I couldn't catch, the fleeting sounds too soft for me to make out, but I got the emotion, "they were angry and fought him, too."

"Did he say anything then?"

"That he had known power like this before."

"Do you know what he meant that time?"

"No."

"What do you know?" he asked. "Think, go over the events in your mind. What can you answer about why you were there when no one else had been before? Why were the whispers angry, and how come they could fight him?"

"They were why," I said, my eyes closed, "we're connected." His questioning brought back the things I knew when we stood in that house, piecemeal and broken as they were. "They won't let anyone separate us."

"What did they do to prevent that?"

"They told me not to let him touch me and then pulled me into the maw -- or I fell into it." A sense I had gone willingly into what they offered me was all I could remember.

"Why couldn't he touch you?"

"He could only steal others' power there, in the house," I said, echoing what the whispers told me. "He was pulling us, our power, into him." With them in my ears, it made it easier to remember what had happened there. "He had to form a -- physical connection between us to do it. But when I went into the maw, there was no power in my body to hold the connection in place, so it severed."

It made my stomach roll again, the realization that all he had needed was to keep some sort of physical contact for the duration it would take for him to absorb someone's power. The torture wasn't necessary; he had done it because he wanted to, because he could.

"That must be the essence," Virgil muttered, then dove into his next set of questions. "What happened when you went into the maw?"

"They caught me, and he was screaming that the gods – those gods – were dead."

Virgil's tone sharpened, "What gods? How does he know they're dead?"

We're not, said the whispers, but the words were there and then gone, and I couldn't be sure I had heard them at all as they faded like a forgotten memory.

"I don't know," I said.

"Could your presence in the house be related to these gods?" he asked.

"I—" I started, but the thought faded again. "No, just the whispers."

He was silent for a long moment, "What happened when you went into the maw? Why did they catch you? Is that what brought you back to your body?"

"No," I said, answering him out of order, "if Bolt hadn't hit me I wouldn't have been able to find my way back. They can't reach me if I'm not in my body, I'm their—" I had to pause and tilt my head to hear what they were telling me, "their anchor. They pulled me into them so he couldn't reach us."

Vengeance, they called, but if it was a name, a want, or a need, I wasn't sure, and so I didn't tell Virgil what they were sighing in my ears.

Virgil put his hand back up at his chin, setting his feet on the floor, but remained seated, watching me. "Again," he said. "From the top."

By the time he was done asking questions and making me repeat myself ad nauseam, I was exhausted. When we left the lab, Greg came striding out of the kitchen to sweep me up. He ignored Virgil and kicked the door to our room closed behind us. I heard it crack.

"You're paying for that!" came Virgil's muffled voice.

Greg set me on the bed, then settled next to me, pulling me against his chest, arms wrapped around me. He was tense under me.

"Are you mad at me?" I asked.

"No."

"You feel mad."

"Not at you."

I tried to squirm away because he was being evasive, and I wanted to look him in the face.

"Please, Meg, just let me hold you."

"Fine," I said. He chuckled at the tone of my voice, although his laugh sounded sad and tired.

CHAPTER TWELVE

We were in the kitchen having coffee the next morning when Virgil came in.

"Did you get the information you needed?" Greg asked him coolly.

"Oh, are you talking to me again?" Virgil asked, not looking up from the phone he was tapping a message on. He pulled out a mug and poured himself a cup of coffee while both hands were still occupied.

"Show off," Greg grunted.

Virgil set his phone down on the counter. "I'm not sure if I did. Meg's power is . . . different." He stood there, sipping coffee while he regarded me over the rim of his cup. "What were your parents like, Meg?"

"Um, normal?"

"What did they do for a living?"

"College professors. History and Mythology," I thought. I hadn't asked much about their day jobs, and they hadn't told me much other than telling me Greek myths and legends at bedtime when I was little.

Virgil's interest sharpened. "Are you not sure, Meg?"

"I don't know."

"Where are you parents now?"

"Same answer: don't know." They had kicked me out when I was eighteen, and I hadn't spoken to them since. I was probably lucky they had waited that long after that night. It might have been kept out of the news, but try explaining to your parents why you wake up every night screaming with figures in your room and they can't get past the door. They wanted nothing to do with it at that point anyway.

"Do your parents exist, Meg?"

"Of course, they exist. Don't ask stupid questions," I snapped. "We just no longer have a relationship."

Virgil subsided for a moment, apparently choosing to ignore my opinion on the subject. "What do you remember about them? What they looked like? Their voices?"

"Virgil," Greg said.

"That they turned out to be assholes, yes and yes. Happy?"

Virgil just grunted.

"Ugh, you," Bolt said, coming in and stepping around Virgil to get to the coffee pot.

"This is my house; I can make you leave if you don't want to be here."

"Hmm, you'd have to catch me first," Bolt said, hoisting herself up onto the kitchen island itself.

"That is Italian Marble you're sitting on."

"And it's oh-so-comfortable."

Greg cleared his throat. "If you two are done with whatever is going on here, I have damage control I need to go do."

"Oh, I already handled that for you," Bolt said.

"What did you tell them?" Greg asked warily.

"That you took the asset to Vigilante for assistance with the trap they were ordering you to set up. And since their order was stupid and high-risk, control of asset was lost, trap failed and said asset was damaged but recovered."

"That is not—"

"What happened? Oh, I know. But now they're busy falling all over themselves to deny they had any involvement in the initial planning and orders. So, you're welcome. You're still gainfully employed." She took a sip of coffee. "Oh, and they want you and the asset back. I told them it still couldn't be moved yet, so I bought you some time before they figure out something is up."

"I may have underestimated you," Virgil said.

"You would."

"Time for what?" I asked.

"To come up with a plan that actually works," Bolt said. "According to the last session of pillow talk, they do not see a reason not to just permanently place the asset under their, uh, protection."

"I definitely underestimated you," Virgil said. "How have you been getting out?"

"I just borrow the remotes for the garage and the gate. I always put them right back on your bedside table when I get back. You talk in your sleep, by the way."

I snorted. Both the men looked at me. "What?" I said. "Obviously you're both too trusting. Keycards, garage remotes. Don't you guys lock up any of your valuables?"

"Normally I don't have guests who go helping themselves to my things," Virgil said.

"Hmm," said Greg.

"Terrible taste in women though," Virgil said, leaving the kitchen.

"Never gonna happen," Bolt called after him.

"What do they mean by permanent protection?" I

asked, hoping they just meant being stuck with a constant babysitter.

"Well, your cell, I mean room, would at least have windows, twenty-four-hour room service, provided you're okay with only three square meals a day," said Bolt.

"They—" I stopped to breathe. "They would—" Greg's hand was on my back again, but he was still listening to Bolt from where she was half twisted to face us, sitting on the island at the cabinet side. But I was focused on the fact that that would be worse than being stuck in Virgil's compound. What if they decided my survival was inconvenient or too dangerous? There was no telling how long it would be before someone took Red Eye down. What if he acquired a power that let him get through walls?

Oh, you're asking about the smoke thing. Yeah, apparently the villain he took that from couldn't get the particles small enough to get through air filtration systems, so the politician's building and Virgil's compound are safe from that kind of attack. Human lungs, though? Some of that villain's kills were messy.

Bolt was speaking again. "They are very afraid of what someone who has already been demonstrably willing to murder civilians would do if they had a power like yours. Not afraid enough to, you know, take care of it before it became a problem. And he's been fairly good about staying under the radar until relatively recently."

At least Bolt was openly sharing what she knew. Greg and I were still working on the fact that he had hidden details from me. And that I had almost attacked him over it. Just because I hadn't sent the whispers after him directly didn't absolve me of anything. You don't just hop back from that. His casual affection with me remained, though, so it would appear we hadn't done any permanent damage to whatever trust we had established. It probably helped that he could hear the truth in my guilt and remorse over it. At some point, we would need to actually talk it out, not slide past it like we were doing.

"How much time did you buy us?" Greg asked.

Bolt shrugged. "Another week at most? Then they're going to want to see you for reassignment."

Greg slid off his stool. "Don't move." He strode out the door. "Virgil, we're on the clock," he yelled down the hallway.

"Where would I go?" I muttered.

"You know he can hear you, right?"

"He's mentioned it a time or two," I said.

Bolt hopped off the counter. "Come on, we should see what the menfolk are trying to plan without us. You know they'll just screw it up."

I followed her out of the kitchen. She headed straight to Virgil's room. It was empty. I paused in the doorway. "Why are we in here?"

She didn't stop, just walked over to a bookcase in the corner and pulled down a bust. "Come on, you can't tell me you didn't think he has secret entrances everywhere?" The bookcase rumbled out of the way, exposing stairs that headed down into darkness.

No, said the whispers. That got my attention.

I watched Bolt steadily. "And they're down there?"

"Obviously."

"I think I'm going to go back to the kitchen and drink my coffee because, stairs," I said apprehensively. "Come tell me what they're screwing up when they're done." I started to turn around, and something slammed into me, knocking me to the ground. I felt the sharp prick of a needle before I could orient myself.

The whispers howled.

I couldn't move; my limbs felt heavy, but someone was lifting me with a grunt.

"I hate dealing with dead weight," Bolt said.

I was floating, and I could feel the figures brushing against me.

Block the doors, I told them, but the shadows were already there.

I stepped away, into the ether with the whispers.

Paint the walls, I told them. But they didn't need to wait for me. They had always acted to protect me in moments I couldn't protect myself.

Then the screams started. She shouldn't have given me drugs. It was going to be that much worse for her now.

∞

"Meg! Meg! Meg, you have to get them to let me in."

I blinked. I was on the floor, staring up at the ceiling where Bolt had dropped me.

I rolled my head towards the door. The figures were still there, standing silently in the way. Their legs extended into the shadows stretching from my body. I was looking at my hand and arm; both were covered in gore and blood. I could feel it sticky and matted in my hair.

"Meg!" The voice insisted. I looked back at the figures, through the inky blackness of them. Greg was on the other side.

Go, I told them, and they came to me, brushing my face with their fingers before they faded away.

Greg was next to me. "Come on, sit up." His arm was behind my back pulling me up. "Let's get you cleaned up, okay?"

He ended up carrying me to the bathroom because the drugs were still in my system, and I couldn't get the coordination to walk right. He set me down against the wall, running the water in the tub.

"Shower." My teeth chattered. I was so cold, cold and tired, and my mind kept wandering, but I had to make sure he knew what I knew from experience. Never take a bath to wash the blood off of you. That ring is never coming out. Or was it that it wasn't going to wash off at all? There was blood floating in the water with me, and like a spot, it wouldn't go. I was there, and then back leaning against a wall, and I wasn't sure which was real. I had something I was supposed to be telling him. "Not the tub."

He stopped what he was doing and looked at me. "Okay," he said gently. He stopped the water in the tub and moved over to the shower. I heard the water start. I closed my eyes and felt myself start to slide against the wall.

Warm hands corrected my course. "Meg, open your eyes. You can't sleep right now."

"Says you."

Hesitation. "Meg, I need to get these clothes off you."

"Okay, but buy a girl dinner first," I giggled. Except I couldn't figure out how to get my arms up so the shirt could come off. There was a sigh, a ripping noise, and then the shirt was gone.

"Wasn't salvageable anyway," a voice said.

I think the pants met the same fate.

Then water hit my back, and I tried to squirm away.

"Don't do that, I don't need to fall in the shower."

"You'd be fine anyway," I snickered.

"But the shower wouldn't be."

He washed my hair.

And stood in the water with me until it ran clear.

He carried me, wrapped up in big fluffy towels, back to our room.

The door to Virgil's room at the end of the hall was shut. I saw it before we went past the door frame into ours.

He settled me on the bed. "Now you can sleep." I dreamt of sand, the sea and olive groves.

∞

There were voices over my head. A tenor, calm and steady, and a baritone, rumbling and warm.

"What happened?"

"I think Bolt slipped her something." The baritone, concern, a plea. Greg? He better not think I murdered her for shits and giggles. I'm not into that.

"Hold on, let me check."

Someone was prying my eyelids open, and I jerked my head back. At least, I tried to. The whispers were there. The hands let go. The whispers faded.

"Okay, not like that." The tenor was wary.

I muttered, turning my face into the pillow.

"What did she say?"

"Syringe."

A door opened. "Well, fuck me." The tenor had moved away, and it was echoing as if the speaker was in a tunnel. The hallway?

I muttered again.

Virgil's voice? From down the hall, "What did she say now?"

"She said she's not paying for that."

A chuckle. A moment of silence. The sound of a door closing.

"Here. Told you we couldn't trust her." The voices were fading, blending together and I couldn't be sure who it was we couldn't trust.

Silence, as the whispers, figures, shadows and I floated among the sand, the sea and an olive grove.

Someone shaking my shoulder. It made my collarbone hurt, and I groaned. "Meg, we're going to need to go. Virgil's worried we're going to end up stuck under siege. He's got the supplies to outlast them, but we can't do anything about Red Eye if we're stuck inside."

"I could make them go away," I grumbled.

"No," Greg said.

"Have it your way." I tried to push away. "I want to sleep."

"Meg, we don't have time. Come on, I've got a shirt for you," he said, and I knew he was right because even though we hadn't seen hide nor hair of Red Eye since my rescue, we knew he was still out there, biding his time. Now we were down a hero, who totally deserved it, but I still felt bad about it. And our situation was about to get worse.

But I couldn't bring myself to let go of that view of the sea.

Greg was pulling the shirt over my head.

"I can dress myself," I snapped, finally opening my eyes. That was a mistake because it made me feel sick. Greg grabbed a trash can and held it in front of me. I pushed it away, breathing in and out while I waited for my stomach to settle. "I thought she said she bought us time."

"She lied. And I missed it," Greg said through gritted teeth. I could hear the guilt and anger in his voice. "Virgil had her apartment bugged. He still won't tell me when he got them in there."

I didn't feel quite so bad about what I had done to her now.

I pulled my arms through the shirt, ignoring the pain. He handed me a pair of pants. I hesitated. There was bruising up and down my legs, as well as spread out in one large blotch from my knee, and I knew, logically, he had already seen the damage done to me that was still healing. I could feel the lines of scar tissue under the bruising both on my legs and my torso. No stitches or evidence of stitches, though, and Virgil won't answer my questions about it. He starts humming. So, despite knowing Greg knew about it, I paused. He turned around so his back was to me. I kicked off the blankets and towels I was still tangled in and pulled the pants on. He pretended not to hear the noises I made struggling into them, but I could tell from the way his muscles tensed.

Healing from torture takes way too long.

I slid my way off the bed, staggered. He caught my waist.

"Are you okay?"

I pushed at his arm. "I would be better if people would stop fucking assaulting me."

"Come on, Virgil's in his garage," he said. "We're going to have to go through his room."

Which meant walking through what was left of Bolt.

"Oh."

He sighed, picked me up, and opened the door to Virgil's room.

The smell hit me, and I gagged. "Jesus," I said, trying to take extra shallow breaths through my mouth.

"Virgil hasn't had a chance to strip the room yet. I think

he's going to just burn it." He floated us over the floor. Because of the low ceilings, he had to do it curled around me, his head bent so that his breath tickled my neck. We reached the door behind the bookcase. "Do you want to walk?"

"Yes." He set me down, and I hurried down the stairs, ignoring the way my knee popped with each movement. I could hear him grinding his teeth again. "You know, you're just gonna have to get used to it," I told him. I was pretty sure some of the damage was going to be permanent. Whenever I asked Virgil about it, he would find a way to change the subject.

"No, what I'm going to do is rip Red Eye limb from limb," he growled.

We had reached the bottom, and Virgil was waiting for us, one arm crossed over his chest, hand on his chin as he considered the two vehicles in front of us.

Right? I would've thought he would have more cars than that too. And I still haven't seen the helicopter.

"Gregor, fast or armored?"

"You don't have one that's both?"

"Okay, let's try this again. Lightly or heavily armored? Heavy is slow."

"Fast."

"Cobra then. In you go."

Greg helped me climb into what there was of a backseat.

The engine roared to life. "You are going to love the modifications I made," Virgil chuckled. He hit the gas, and the tires squealed as the car leapt forward. The sound it made as it went up the tunnel was deafening. Then we were out and speeding down toward the gate.

"The gate," Greg said.

"Keep your hair on," Virgil told him.

The gate was opening too slowly, but with a protesting

squeal it slammed back out of the way. Virgil almost clipped the side mirror on it as we went through. "Hmm, timing a shade off," he said. Behind us, we could hear the gate protest again as it slammed shut.

"Hey," I said from the back seat. "Try to remember I break easily. You know, before you wreck your toy."

Virgil chuckled again. "I don't wreck."

Greg had one arm braced on the ceiling, the other on the dash. "I take it back, slow would be better."

The tires squealed as Virgil drifted us around a curve. "If you put dents in my car, I will kick you out on the side of the road, and you can fly the rest of the way."

The car bounced, and I slammed into the side as we took another curve. I yelped.

"Damn it, Virgil."

"Meg, get buckled," Virgil said.

"I am buckled!" I yelled at him. "It only does so much when you drive like that; there's no shoulder harness!" Although, to be honest, I don't know that it would've actually helped. I needed a five-point harness if I didn't want to get tossed around like I was.

"Do not try to climb back there while I'm driving," Virgil said, and Greg glared at him.

I was glad I was mostly out of it the last time Virgil drove me anywhere.

"Watch the road," Greg said.

"I am watching the road."

"Cows," Greg said. "Those are cows. COWS!"

There were startled, bellowing moos as the cows were shoved to either side of the road and the car slid through the gap Virgil had created.

I looked behind us. The cows were tripping all over

themselves to get the rest of the way off the road and get space between them and whatever had just happened.

"I love country life," Virgil said.

∞

Eventually the roads Virgil was following spit us out onto a major highway. His driving there wasn't much better, but at least the road was mostly straight, so I wasn't getting thrown around.

Greg was keeping an eye out the windows. The three of us, now that I was being included in the discussions, had come to the conclusion that there was a high likelihood that Red Eye would follow us now that I was on the move. Since I had already demonstrated an aptitude for wandering off on my own, it was likely he would assume I might be stupid enough to do it again.

Look, we've already had this conversation about my survival instincts. I tend to let the dramatics of the moment overrule the "don't die" plan.

"Relax. He's not going to be able to follow us at this speed," Virgil said. He slid the car through a gap in traffic, had to tap the brakes. The car in front of us bumped forward a bit. "I need these people to get out of the way."

"Do not shove their car again."

"I didn't even do it enough to be noticed. Just so I wasn't right on their bumper. Look, their car would fit right behind that one; they won't even know it wasn't something they did."

Greg glared at him.

Virgil sighed. "Meg, back me up here."

"Uh uh," I said. "You're on your own."

"Sticks in the mud, both of you," Virgil muttered.

Fortunately, the car took the opportunity to get out of the way without his intervention, and Virgil gassed it, flying up the now-clear lane. I peeked up front; the speedometer had topped out at 160, and we were coming up on more cars.

Greg was pushing back against his seat; I could hear it creak.

"Would you relax?" Virgil said. "We're coming up on our exit anyway." He put action to his words pulling the steering wheel to the right. His car shot across the lanes, bounced, and we were speeding down the ramp.

"That's a red light," Greg said.

"Yup, just hold on. Um, might want to steady Meg."

Greg twisted and lunged so his top half was in the back, his arm braced against me.

Virgil yanked the emergency brake up. The tires squealed as he took the corner, and we fishtailed when he released the brake and hit the gas. He flicked a hand, and the car steadied. Behind us horns were blaring.

Virgil finally slowed to the speed limit once we were a few streets down. "Gregor, you've got to sit back. I can't see around you." He was taking us further into a "New Main Street America" kind of town, winding down the streets, where suburbia was still only a couple blocks from downtown. The kind where you knew if you went just a bit further out you would start finding the strip malls that were killing the mom-and-pop stores. Oh look, there's one now.

Greg twisted back, sitting down hard enough that the car itself groaned.

"That wasn't necessary," Virgil said. He was leaning forward, angling his face to read the street signs we were passing. "Keep an eye out for White Oleander. I've only been here once before."

"There," Greg said.

Virgil used his turn signal for once, and then we were rumbling down neighborhood streets, passing cookie cutter houses and yards, bright with flowers and well-kept grass.

"Jesus," I said. "Little bit Stepford wives-esque."

"Not into the picket fence, two-and-a-half kids plus a dog kind of life, Meg?" Virgil asked.

"Dogs don't like me," I said. Or the whispers didn't like dogs. Dogs wouldn't come near me whether I was using my power or not. I wasn't even touching the comment on kids. I don't need to be responsible for screwing up a tiny human and sending them off into the world. Do I look like kids should be in the cards for me?

He finally pulled up and parked in front of a house that looked like all the others; the only difference was the numbers on the mailbox. 1180. "We're here, everybody out." Virgil hopped out and headed for the front door. He was knocking on the door while Greg helped me out. I heard it open.

"Vigilante," came the wary, vaguely familiar voice. I was trying to place it, but the whispers were pulling at me, agitated.

"Calling in a favor, need a hide out for a couple days," Virgil was telling him when the man caught sight of me coming out of the car.

"Oh no, no, she cannot come in here." The voice clicked, and I looked up. Brown hair, thin, lanky build, smarmy smug expression mixed with panic? Check, check and check.

"What the fuck?!" I shouted.

"Hi, Meg," Mirage said weakly.

"You were dead!" I said, still trying to process this.

"Surprise?" he said, giving his hands a halfhearted "ta-da" wave.

I charged him. At least I tried to. But Greg caught me and placed his body between us. "You fucker! You cost me my security deposit!" I was trying to claw my way around Greg ignoring the way it pulled at my collarbone, although the sound I made when it did wasn't entirely human. Greg lifted me up, clamping his arms around me.

"Meg!" he said.

"I will literally tear you apart myself this time!" I snarled. Except I couldn't get myself free. Greg had me pinned against him so I couldn't move, which might have been as much to prevent me from hurting myself as it was to prevent me from hurting Mirage. The whispers were swirling around and calling me, but I wouldn't let them out because I was too close to Greg, and I had promised him.

Virgil cleared his throat. "We need to get inside."

"Oh no, no," Mirage was protesting, but Greg had shouldered him aside, I tried to kick my feet back at him as we went by, but Greg swung me away, and Virgil snapped the door shut behind us.

"Sounds like you might owe Meg an explanation," Virgil said, sounding almost cheerful.

"Yeah, like why you're not dead!" I shouted, twisting as much as I could to face him. It made my collarbone ache. I stayed that way anyway.

"I might have, um, paid someone to break into your apartment. And, uh, illusion powers..." he pulled at his shirt collar.

"You what?! Who did I kill?" Jesus, had I murdered someone who thought it was a prank or something? Now that I thought about it, the way he acted, and his facial expressions had been slightly off that night, but I had chalked it up to him finally escalating to breaking into my apartment to potentially rape and murder me.

Mirage was pulling at his shirt collar. "Well, I mean, I knew he was a criminal, but I didn't realize he uh, had been in jail for—" he cleared his throat. "Glad you didn't get hurt," he finished lamely.

"Why would you do that?" I was still yelling. Two years this asshole had harassed me, showing up in the middle of the night, leaving creepy shit on my doorstep, and now he was here, apparently not dead.

"I was trying to get out? And you know, you don't just retire from the villain life. So, I might have used you to fake my own death?"

"Put me down, Greg," I growled because as soon as Greg set me down, I wasn't even going to need the whispers because I was going to tear Mirage's eyes out with my own hands.

"I don't know that I should," Greg said.

"Oh, you definitely should," I snapped.

"Does it help if I tell you the maggots weren't real?" Mirage asked.

"No, it doesn't fucking help!" I yelled. I turned on Virgil as well as I could from where I was pressed against Greg. Let me tell you, it's hard to look scary angry when you have to keep swiveling your face past someone's chest. "And you! How did you know about this? Did you help him?"

"Oh no, he did that all on his own. I came in after the fact," Virgil said.

"Hey, yeah, this is blackmail by the way, and I would like you to leave please," Mirage said.

"Fortress, put Meg down," Virgil said. For a moment I was confused until I was realized Virgil was using their hero names around Mirage.

"Whoa, wait, wait, wait, man! It's fine, we're cool, mi casa es su casa," Mirage said, his hands up.

"Good to hear," Virgil said. "We need your help with a little project."

"I'm sorry, I draw the line at actively helping my blackmailers," Mirage stopped and cleared his throat at the look Virgil gave him. "I mean, yeah, sure, what do you need man?"

"An illusion," Virgil said.

CHAPTER THIRTEEN

Virgil had insisted everyone sit down while he told us what he had planned. Greg had sat down on the couch, pinning me against his side.

"I'm not going to do anything," I grumbled. He ignored me, probably because he knew I was lying.

Virgil was questioning Mirage on the strength of the illusions he cast.

"Well, yeah, man, I can layer it right down to the bone. That's why the pathologist didn't notice that—" he looked up at me. "Anyway, yeah. They're tight. Really accurate. Solid, you know."

"Why me?" I asked.

"Why you what?" Mirage asked.

"Why did you pick me? Why didn't you just go pull that shit on one of the villains? They would've killed your lackey a lot sooner."

"Because you're you."

"That literally answers nothing," I snapped at him. "You stalked me for two years!"

I felt Greg's hand tense against my side, his fingers

flexing. I looked up at his face. His jaw was tight, and he was watching Mirage with a hard stare. I set my hand on his thigh, and he looked down at me, surprised. His muscles relaxed, and he leaned back into the couch. I turned my attention back to Mirage but left my hand on Greg's leg.

"Two years," I said again.

Virgil was watching us with interest. "You should just answer Meg's question. It'll clear the air and make working together easier on everyone."

I bet Virgil only took my side because he was curious and wanted to know the motivation behind it even more than I did. Because I doubt he cared about Mirage's feelings on working with a couple heroes. And whatever I count as.

Mirage sighed. "Because everyone knows what you can do, Meg, and I needed my death to be convincing. Look, I'm sorry. I had to draw it out a little bit, otherwise it wouldn't be believable. And everyone knew you were undecided, so trying to woo you to our side would've been reasonable. But, you know, in a creepy way, so eventually you would get fed up and murder me. I honestly didn't expect it to take two years. I thought, like, six months tops." He gave an uncomfortable laugh. "I mean, I had to take it to extremes before you would do anything other than use your power to make my fakes bugger off."

"You tried to make me murder random people just so you could retire," I said flatly.

"I mean, okay, yeah, when you put it that way it sounds bad. But . . .villain?"

"You're an asshole."

"Villain," Mirage corrected.

Virgil clapped his hands together. "Well, I think we're done here."

"Oh, good, so you're leaving?" Mirage said.

"Oh no. No, we've still got more planning to do. The therapy session is done. We need a location where there won't be any civilian casualties. We need somewhere open, unpopulated. What's outside of town?"

"Man, I don't fucking know. You think I ever took that into consideration before?" Mirage said.

"Any dying shopping centers? Movie theaters?" Virgil asked.

"Well, there was a drive in. Oh, that's outside town. It's abandoned. Sad, too, man, they had the best popcorn. Like, would really load on the butter."

"Address?" Virgil asked, pulling out his phone.

"Off Highway 9."

Virgil was tapping, studying what he found. "Fortress, lay of the land. Tell me where you need to be." He handed the phone over to Greg.

I leaned my head against Greg's shoulder, studying the satellite image Virgil had pulled up. Greg tapped a spot and handed the phone back over. "There. Front and center."

Virgil studied it, frowning. "That's out in the open. You think he's going to rush it?"

"I'm counting on it."

"Eggs, basket," Virgil said.

"You just get everything set up and let me worry about the basket."

"I think you're supposed to worry about the eggs," said Mirage.

"How long will the illusion last?" Virgil interrupted before Greg and Mirage could get into an argument about the semantics of it.

"Oh, until I release it. So, just call me when you're done

with it."

"Oh no, you're going to need to be there. Release signal is going to need line of sight."

"Look man," he quailed at the look Greg shot him. "Yeah, sure, whatever you say. Just don't get me killed, alright?" Well, that made me feel smug. Because with Red Eye being as dangerous as he is, Mirage might just die anyway.

Look, I'm kind of vindictive. What do you want from me? Oh, like you wouldn't be if you were in this situation.

"Great, all set?" Virgil asked. "Lovely, so what are we thinking? Chinese?"

"What about curry?" Greg suggested.

Mirage snorted. "Look, I don't know what kind of fancy pants town you all think I settled in, but here we have pizza and burgers. Pick one of those."

"What kind of burgers?" Greg asked.

"What do you mean what kind of burgers? Burger burgers. Used to moo? Burgers, man."

"Pizza?" Virgil asked.

"Pizza," Greg said.

∞

Mirage didn't have any extra bedrooms.

Well, that wasn't entirely true. He had a three-bedroom house. One room was his (and no way was I sleeping in there, gross, even if he had offered it, which he hadn't), one he had set up as an office, and the last was apparently an art studio.

You know who else tried his hand at being an artist? Hitler. So don't go getting all "Mirage can't be all that bad if he paints."

Virgil ended up running into town to get air mattresses,

extra sheets, blankets and pillows from a Wal-Mart. Before he left, he spent several minutes quizzing Mirage on what kind of defenses his house had. When he got back, he parked his car in the driveway this time, front facing the street, and floated everything in rather than wasting time making trips while Mirage hissed at him not to let the neighbors see because he didn't need some dumbass talking to the wrong people about the hero next door.

"You're gonna blow my cover and get me killed," he complained for the next ten minutes.

Virgil finally got irritated. "Just lock the fucking house down." When Mirage walked off to the controls for the house, conveniently disguised as a fuse box, Virgil turned to me. "Meg, you want the art gallery or the office space?"

"Office space," Greg and I said at the same time.

Virgil cleared his throat. "I was asking Meg, so you two can work that out between you."

Greg just grabbed a set of the bedding and one of the air mattresses and stalked off to the office. I followed him and leaned against the wall just inside the room.

He was sitting on the floor, unboxing the air mattress and getting it unfolded.

"So," I said, "You done trying to make all the decisions for me yet?"

He sighed, scrubbed at his face. "The office is the bedroom with the least exposure."

"Hmm, I just wanted it because it didn't have any of that shitty art in it."

He chuckled. "Well at least we ended up on the same page even if it was by different routes." He twisted back to look up at me. "You know, you don't have to forgive him. You just have to stomach working with him."

"Hmm," I said, to keep from saying what I wanted to say. Or admitting that I had seriously considered making sure Mirage was actually dead if we survived the coming day. Greg and Virgil had spent time arguing it, but in the end, there hadn't been a choice. My presence was going to be required to draw Red Eye into the trap they were setting up.

Virgil was convinced he was following me through my dreams, or at least it had started that way. He wasn't sure if his power to cause nightmares had always been there, or if something about me had made his powers evolve. We might never know the answer to that. It had Virgil in knots with plans for future research, but I had never been one to investigate mysterious circumstances, and that wasn't about to change anytime soon.

Once this was over, if we lived, I was going to go straight back to my boring, quiet life. Albeit minus a job. And I might have to move. Or go on the lam for a bit. I hadn't planned much about the whole "murdered a hero" thing. But if that happened, at least the hero recruitment wouldn't be a thing anymore. And Greg had promised to get them off my back completely after this, doing his best to sound convinced we would all come out of this unscathed.

He and Virgil had appeared so confident that this plan would work, but I had felt the tension in the air, felt the way Greg's muscles had bunched together where I had sat, still pinned to his side on the couch. I didn't have it in me to tell him I knew he had doubts. Although maybe he knew I knew. He could probably hear it in my heartbeat.

He had turned back to the air mattress, so I crouched down next to him. "Want some help?"

He stopped what he was doing and looked me in the eye. "Meg—" he started, and then stopped. He started again. "Meg, if, if it looks like things are going badly tomorrow, run. You have to promise me you'll run."

"No," I said.

His hands were on my face. "Meg, I need to focus. I can't focus if I'm worried you'll put yourself in danger. Please, please, promise me you'll run. If I go down, you need to run."

"Okay," I said, and then I kissed him because I didn't want him to hear the lie in the beat of my heart. I didn't wait for him to pull me toward him, I climbed in his lap, wrapping my legs around his waist.

He reached back and shut the door with a slam. The wood groaned.

"Lock it," I murmured, my lips pressed against his.

He chuckled. "Oh, it's embedded in the frame. They're not coming in."

He wrapped his arms around me, pulling me in tight, and then his hands were warm against the skin of my back as he slid them under my shirt.

I let go of him to lift my shirt off, then hissed when the motion pulled on my collarbone. He stilled against me.

"You're still healing."

"I'm fine," I insisted.

He hesitated. I yanked the shirt off, biting back against the pain. "There, now it's off."

This time, he didn't hesitate, his hands on my ribs, fingers brushing the underside of my breasts, and then his lips were on mine. I tugged at his shirt, and with a chuckle, he pulled it off one-handed, the other against the small of my back.

He pulled me back in against him, chest to chest, and I could feel his heart beating in time with mine.

His lips were against my neck, his breath tickling my skin, and I gasped at the shiver it sent down my spine.

209

"We don't have a bed yet," he murmured.

"I don't care."

He chuckled, and then rose to his knees, tilting me back onto the bedding piled on the floor. "Close enough," he said, pressing back against me. My fingers were in the waistband of his jeans, pulling at them, so he yanked and kicked them off, and I could hear the fabric tear.

"Damn it," he said, and I giggled. "Oh, is that funny?" he asked me.

"Yes," I said, still giggling.

"Maybe I'll just do the same to yours," he said. I was pinned beneath him, his hands on my waist, one working its way down the back of my pants.

"Wouldn't be the first time," I quipped at him, and he paused, looking down at me, eyes suddenly serious. I reached up to touch his face. "I'm fine," I told him, and he kissed me.

He was very gentle when he finally got around to my pants.

∞

He was drawing circles on my back in the dark after. His fingers brushed over my skin, soothing in their warmth.

"Meg," he said.

"Hmm?" I said. Because I wanted to sleep, but I was worried he would remind me to run again. He had sounded so desperate when he asked me to promise him.

"Virgil told me to tell you," he said bitterly. "He told me to tell you the truth about Red Eye almost from the start."

I lifted my head even though I wasn't ready to have this conversation. I was hoping it would wait until we found out if we were living or dying. Because if we died, we could skip it entirely. But he was choosing to, and I wouldn't ask him to wait if he needed this. As much as I hate having these kinds of talks. And this time, at least I hadn't led us into it.

"How long?" I asked, after the silence had stretched.

"He knew before we went to him for help that Red Eye was hunting someone. I didn't tell him it was you until we were there."

He was silent again, and even if I wanted to, I'm not the kind of person who can make confession and absolution easy on people. Not even on myself. So I waited, even though it made my shoulder blades itch to do so. Almost absent mindedly, he moved his fingers up, so they were gently scratching at the itch.

Hmm, I'm going to have to work on my poker face. Poker heart?

"After you were asleep," he sighed, scrubbing at his face with his free hand, "he told me I had to tell you what Red Eye could do. That if I didn't give you all the information, if I hid it from you, you wouldn't react well."

Didn't take long for Virgil to get my number, did it?

"And I was going to, I swear, but you woke up, and you had had that nightmare, and the next morning—" there was a plea in his voice, "I couldn't get my footing around you. And I couldn't add to the stress you were under. I kept finding a reason to delay it."

I didn't say anything, because I hadn't been honest from the start either. I was still hiding things. If we lived, eventually I would have to explain the extent of what I could do. He might have an idea of my power from my file, but it didn't tell the whole story.

That I could hear the sea in my ears, even if I didn't know what it meant.

"Meg," he said, "please say something."

"I'm sorry, too," was all I said. Because I was. I had let things build until they came to a boiling point, and I had lashed out at him in a way that was unacceptable, no matter what the reasons were at the time.

And I was lucky in that moment that he was a better person than I was, because I don't know that I would have rescued me.

"I wanted to protect you," he said, "but you had already told me you could rescue yourself, and I ignored that."

"So next time, don't," I told him.

"Will you stop flinging yourself into danger when I piss you off?"

"That's your takeaway?" I said, incredulous. "Not the part where I freaked out and went after you and Virgil?"

"I already knew you did that kind of thing."

"I'm sorry, are you making excuses for me?" I twitched my shoulders, moving away from him.

He made a frustrated noise. "No, I'm not. You—" He was shoving his hair out of his face; we were still close enough that my night vision was good. "I've seen what happens with your power and your emotions, and I should have warned Virgil. He wouldn't have pushed at you the way he did otherwise."

"I practically attacked you," I said slowly. I was surprised at his level of observation about the whispers, although I supposed I shouldn't have been.

"No, you lost control. You never actually sent them after me. You absolutely attacked Virgil, though, so you might want to apologize to him." He thought for a minute. "And definitely work on your self-control."

I opened my mouth to protest again - his viewpoint of

the situation or my lack of control, I wasn't sure which, maybe both. But he sighed, and it made me hesitate. "We both made mistakes. I can move past this one," he said.

"Okay," I said.

"Okay?" he asked.

"Okay," I said.

He pulled me back toward him, his lips on mine with a quiet kind of urgency to his touch. And I gave myself over to it, because for a while we could both forget what waited for us.

CHAPTER FOURTEEN

Virgil and Greg spent part of the morning arguing over whether we were all going in his car or if Greg was flying me in. Mirage said he could drive his own car, but Virgil had told him they weren't stupid enough to fall for that offer.

Eventually we all ended up squishing into Virgil's Cobra. Greg had planted me in the seat behind the driver, then climbed in next to me. Mirage had hesitated about climbing into the passenger side, so Virgil had "assisted" him in.

"Ow, man! Damn, dude, you didn't need to do that! I just didn't want to be sitting in front of Fortress." Mirage jerked back when Virgil shut the car door in his face.

"I would've thought you would be more worried about what I might do to you," I said. By the way, it's hard to look like anything other than a pissed off kitten when you're squished up because there's no space.

Mirage twisted to look back at me. "Look, have you seen what this dude can do? I don't want to be in a car with either of you. This is, like, my worst nightmare."

I smirked at him.

"At least if Vigilante kills me, it'll be quick," Mirage muttered, turning back toward the front.

"No, it won't," Virgil said, climbing into his seat. He shut the door, and the car roared to life.

Mirage's eyes widened. "Oh, sweet. What kind of engine did you modify this with?"

"Wouldn't you like to know?" Virgil said as he pulled out onto the street.

"Look, man, you came to me for help. You could at least be, like, polite or some shit."

"This is about as polite as he gets," Greg said.

Mirage muttered something about us all being ungrateful.

"I can hear that," Greg told him.

Mirage tucked his head down and didn't say anything for the rest of the ride to the drive-in. Honestly, with the way Virgil drives, I wasn't talking either.

Virgil parked his car back behind the concession stands, hiding it as well as he could in the overgrown bushes.

Mirage tried the door to the concession stands, jiggling the handle. It didn't open. "Oh, damn, locked. Guess this isn't going to work." He started to turn around. Greg caught his shoulder, reached for the handle with his free hand and twisted. The lock popped and the door swung free.

"Now it's not," Greg said.

We all went in. Greg and Virgil got the rolling door at the front counter cracked open and set so it would stay that way. Either one of them could have handled it on their own, but the cooperation between them had happened so automatically it made me wonder how many times they had worked together before. Now that we were past the planning stage and at the business end of the mission, they were working smoothly together. Any arguments or disagreements were put away and forgotten, at least temporarily. It made why they were friends more clear to me. Although I suppose it should have been clear to me from the start when the first person Greg turned to for help wasn't another hero in the same building.

"Do you have a clear view through this?" Greg asked Mirage.

Mirage crouched, chin on the interior counter. "Yeah, man, view is good. I can see the whole lot."

Virgil shut the door we came in through with a wave of his hand. "Good, then let's get started before he notices we've changed locations."

Mirage looked at the three of us. "Look, I need privacy? Just uh, Fortress and me in here."

"Performance anxiety?" Virgil asked. He planted himself in front of the door. "I would've thought having the model in front of you would be helpful."

Mirage muttered but got to work. "I'm, uh, going to need to touch you," he said to me. "It'll go faster that way."

"Fine," I said, and he reached out to put his fingers on my face. I closed my eyes because he was too close to me, and I didn't want to be staring into his eyes. My heart sped up.

"Meg," Greg said.

"I'm fine," I snapped.

"Hold still, man! You moving around makes it harder to layer this shit. You want it to look all janky?"

I could hear Greg grinding his teeth again.

Mirage took his fingers off my face. "Done. Will hold up to scrutiny even under death. Well, I mean, except for when they try to move the body because no way you would weigh the same. I can't do anything about actual physicality. The dude I—" he stopped at the look on my face. He cleared his throat.

"We were pretty close in actual resemblance, so, yeah. Sorry about that." He moved away from me.

I looked over at Greg, to find my face staring back at me. "Oh, wow. That is…" I had to stare, fascinated, because having a doppelganger is just freaky.

"Uncanny," Virgil finished for me. We all stared at the not-me-Meg for a moment.

"Stop staring, we need to finish getting set up." Greg's voice coming out of my mouth just made it weirder.

"Yup." Virgil turned to me, pressing his car keys in my hand. "If things go south, I'm covering you until you get out. Hit the home button, the car will know what to do."

I hadn't been expecting that. I could hear Greg shift behind me. "Does it drive like you do?" I asked, my muscles tense, heart hammering from nerves, and I was trying to cover that I had no intention of following through on running. I could remember the scent of salt in the air and a sense of something I was, or had once been, and that memory wouldn't let me do anything but fling myself into danger.

See, I have more reasons for doing that than just spite.

Virgil just chuckled. Then he went out the door, me-Greg following him, one warm hand brushing my shoulder before he left, except where his me-hand hovered was nowhere near where my shoulder was. They closed the door behind them, and then I was left in the concession stand with Mirage.

He cleared his throat. "So, Meg, when did you become a hero?"

"I didn't," I said.

"Okay, whatever you say, man." Mirage lay his upper half across the counter, peering out the crack in the rolling door.

I was still clutching Virgil's keys in my hand. I stashed

them in the back pocket of my jeans and joined Mirage at the counter. Being next to him made my skin crawl, but I couldn't stand not knowing what was happening out there.

Greg as not-me-Meg was in the middle of the cracked and weed-choked pavement of what used to be the lot with the old screen off to his left and his back to us at the concession stands. He was watching the sky, slowly turning in place. I couldn't see where Virgil was, which meant he was already hidden, down among the undergrowth surrounding the back of the screen.

Outside, I could hear birds singing. The occasional rustle in the grass that had grown up around the stand. It would've been a nice location if we had been here for a different reason. It felt peaceful.

Maybe Red Eye wouldn't come. Maybe he had given up hunting me.

But I'd had nightmares last night.

The birds went quiet. The rustling in the grass stopped.

Something heavy landed on the roof of our stand, and I heard a scraping sound like claws on wood. I shuddered at the sound, silently praying that he didn't look beyond the obvious. Mirage turned his face to mine, one finger held up against his lips. I glared back at him. He shrugged his shoulders, as he sliced a finger across his throat and pointed up, then mimed zipping his lips. I rolled my eyes, turning back to the crack. He did the same, and we both stared out at not-me-Meg, who had turned to face the stand.

Not-me-Meg flipped off the thing on top of the concession stand.

It was a totally me thing to do. When I'm not, you know, terrified I'll die.

There was a shriek, and the roof above us groaned as

Red Eye took off, leathery wings beating, and he dove for not-me, who stood her ground.

Red Eye got a surprise when he reached not me.

Greg's quite a bit taller than I am, and while it looked like me, Greg's body still takes up the same amount of space. Which means his reach is also quite a bit longer.

Mirage reached a hand out into thin air and pulled.

Greg wrenched Red Eye out of the air and slammed him down into the paving of the lot. Then he was over Red Eye, his fist headed for the thing's chest.

It poofed into smoke, and Greg's fist slammed into the pavement. I could feel the ground shake from the impact.

Red Eye re-formed a few feet away, facing Greg, crouched in human form. "Where is she?" it snarled at him.

Greg didn't answer him.

For a moment, they both stood still.

And then they charged each other. Red Eye had shifted into the huge, black dog-like thing, and he leapt at Greg, who twisted, grabbing it out of the air and throwing it at the old screen.

The thing turned to smoke and then re-formed, once again standing on the pavement.

Still too far from the spot marked X.

They charged each other again, and this time, they slammed into each other, grappling.

Have you ever watched one of those nature documentaries, and you see a couple Grizzly bears get in a fight? The way they rip into each other? Yeah, same energy. Go, watch one right now so you can see what I'm talking about. I'll wait.

Seeing something like that in person is terrifying. They were tearing, snarling, Red Eye half shifted, fangs gnashing in

Greg's face, who was planted like a tree, leaned into Red Eye, his feet literally digging furrows into the pavement as Red Eye pushed back against him.

Red Eye switched tactics, poofing into smoke to avoid Greg's grasp and working to turn his strength back against him. Some of the hardest hits looked like they ended up doing no more damage than a love tap would when Greg's fists would actually land.

But Red Eye was distracted, and Greg was working him back over to the screen.

This time Red Eye made a mistake.

Greg hit him, and Red Eye reeled back from the blow, staggering.

I heard the snapping of wood as the screen started to fall.

Greg leapt out of the way, and hundreds of pounds of plywood and two by fours landed on Red Eye.

Greg waited at the edge, wary.

Virgil popped out from the undergrowth. "Did I get him?" he yelled.

Greg waved a hand in a shushing movement. The look on his face told me something about this had been too easy.

There was smoke coming up out of an empty knot in the wood.

"Fuck," Virgil said.

Red Eye re-formed, standing on top of what was left of the screen. "I grow weary of this," he growled.

"Villains and their dramatics," Virgil said.

There was the groan of wood, and a sheet of the plywood pulled free, headed straight for Red Eye. It changed course, spinning around him instead of into him, and headed for Virgil, who was too close to get out of the way.

"Oh fuck—" it hit Virgil, who went flying. He hit the ground, rolled as the piece of plywood bounced away and rose with a stagger.

Greg had already re-engaged, slamming a shoulder into Red Eye as he bound his arms around him. Red Eye simply snarled, seeming to elongate as he reached over and around to grab Greg by the stomach and lift him bodily into the air. Greg clawed at him, upside down, and clamped his hands onto one of Red Eye's legs, and then the two of them slammed into the ground as Greg yanked the leg up and Red Eye tilted backwards. The wood of the concession stand vibrated as the ground shook from the impact.

Red Eye was digging his own talons into Greg, who gave a surprised yell as he scrambled to pull free. I saw the flash of raised welts on his arm, and then Red Eye went sliding across the pavement, ripped away from Greg. One of Red Eye's hands came up as he snarled again and pulled at the air. Virgil went flying again, slamming hard into the pavement on the other side of the lot.

Greg was back on his feet and had Red Eye in another bear hug, his arms tightening. I could see the cords of his muscles bulging, but a second later the strength apparent seemed to melt away as Red Eye simply stepped out of his grip, snagged one of his arms and threw him. Mirage and I scrambled away from the window to duck and cover. We heard the crash and splinter of wood as Greg landed on the stand next to the one we were hiding in.

I was back at the window in time to see Virgil, who must have gotten to his feet while Red Eye was busy with Greg, go flying again, this time crashing into the underbrush and bushes where the screen used to stand. There was a clattering noise as Greg fought free of the remnants of the stand. He chased after

Red Eye who kept sliding out of his reach.

Mirage was pulling at my arm. "We need to go, like, now."

I yanked my arm away. "Fuck off," I hissed at him. I was trying to see what was happening.

He grabbed at me again. "Give me the fucking keys!"

I hit him with the fear, and he screamed and ran for the door. I was back at the gap in the rolltop as soon as he had released me, letting the whispers chase after him. The panic they were creating caused him to run into the door instead of remembering to open it. He hit it hard, too; the solid crack sounded like he might have broken his nose. He staggered back and fell to the floor stunned.

The noise was more than enough to attract attention.

Red Eye looked straight at the booth.

Greg tackled him, and then they were grappling and ripping at each other again. Red Eye grabbed Greg's arm as he dodged a hit. There was a crack like a gunshot, and Greg screamed, staggering back, clutching at his arm.

Red Eye was pressing his advantage, snarling and shifting between human and dog, bearing down on Greg, who was sidestepping out of the way, his injured arm held pressed against his stomach.

Greg had an opening, and he took it, fist flying. Red Eye ducked, a swift sliding motion, and came up with a hit to Greg's ribs. I could actually see them bow inward even as another crack split the air.

Greg fell, crumpling to the ground between one breath and the next.

I screamed, and the whispers and figures were at my back, their long fingers pulling open the door.

I ran, the shadows stretching before me, rising, dark and

terrible in their rage.

We surged over the lot straight at Red Eye, the whispers howling in glee, figures swirling, slamming into him. He shrieked in terror.

And then I was on him, furious. This time, I touched his face, my fingers headed for those eyes.

∞

Between one breath and the next.

∞

And we were in the house, as familiar to me as the back of my hand.

The stairs in the entryway that led up to the bedrooms. The den to the right, filled with books on heavy bookcases. The living room to my left, warm and inviting, big windows, sunlight, thick carpeting. The couches were white.

I knew if I continued through, I would find the kitchen and dining room. Open and airy. And behind them, the deck and the garden. Swing in an oak tree.

It had been picturesque.

And I had ruined it and all those lives.

Did I tell you I was the one who threw the party while my parents were out of town for some conference or other?

No? Well, now you know.

It was my own fault in more ways than one that so many people died that night. All of it hinged on my choices.

I might be lucky not to be more messed up than I am. Because remember, drugs and I don't get along. I ended up lying in the remains for a day before anyone realized something was wrong. You would think the neighbors would've noticed the screaming. Or the sudden lack thereof once my vocal cords had given out since I was the last to stop.

Check on your neighbors, folks, they might be high out of their minds covered in the blood and guts of a few dozen teenagers.

The whispers were pulling at me, figures brushing against my back and shoulders. They laughed and told me that he was here. They had brought him to me. To the place where I had first embraced what we could do.

I followed them to the living room.

Red Eye was standing there, slowly turning as he took in the room. He stopped, looking at me.

"What did you do to me?" he snarled.

I shrugged. Because I hadn't done it, the whispers had.

He shrieked and leapt at me. But the figures were in the way, and they slammed into him. He staggered back and stared at his arm in shock.

Rips had opened in his skin. But he hadn't done it to himself.

I could feel the fury in the whispers, the rage in the figures. They wanted torment. All I had to do was open myself fully to them. Like I had done at the party, like I had done to Bolt. So I let them in. Or maybe I already had, when I chose to remember and accepted what we were capable of together.

Greg was right. I was underutilizing what I could do.

I reached out, brushing my fingers against Red Eye's hand where he still stood, staring at the blood. Because now, we could tear his essence from him, part of our vengeance.

∞

And then we were back in the lot of the drive-in, and he was screaming as I hammered the fear and the fury into him. He was trying to scramble back from me, but the whispers were relentless, laughing in his ears as the figures pulled off strips of his skin, their long fingers burrowing into the exposed flesh. The shadows and I dogged him, blocking his path so he couldn't flee from us.

He screamed, ripping at himself as he tried to get them off, but there was nothing there for him to grab. They swirled around him, and as he tried to yank the power from me, they billowed and dove into him again.

He squealed, ripping chunks of muscle free and tried to push back against them, send them fleeing. They rippled in the air, the shadows stretching, bending back.

"*No*," the whispers and I screamed.

They tore into him.

This time he couldn't touch the power behind them.

Even after his screams faded, the figures didn't stop, the whispers giggling until there was nothing left but a glistening pile of sinew and bone.

There was a sickening pop, and his head rolled free. It stopped, facing me, the skin and eyes gone, a gaping hole where the mouth should have been.

Silence.

I stood among the figures, the shadows and the whispers as they swirled around me. Waiting.

Movement to my left. I turned to face it, the figures swirling with me, curling against my shoulders.

Virgil, hands up, palms out. He was sweating. "Meg," he said, "you need to tell them to go. I can't reach Greg."

Greg.

I pulled them to me, and they came, leaving the circle they had formed around him. I hadn't told them to do that.

Virgil rushed over to him, his hands over Greg's body where he lay. He was so still.

"Fuck, fuck, fuck," Virgil was muttering.

I took a step toward them. Virgil staggered, away, shuddering. I stopped moving.

"Go wait in the car, Meg," he said.

"No," I said, the whispers howling.

"I cannot help him if you're here with them. So either get some fucking control or wait in the car!"

I took a breath. Stifled a sob. The figures brushed my face, and then the whispers left.

Virgil was back at Greg's side. "Come on," he was muttering.

I crept over, and this time Virgil didn't freak out, he just ignored me, still concentrating on Greg's body. My stomach rolled; Greg's side and chest looked like it had been caved in. His shirt settled and clung to the hollow shape of it. There were black spots in my vision, and I couldn't breathe.

"Meg!" Virgil's voice. "Don't you dare pass out. I need you to talk to him." He was pulling me, shoving me over to Greg's other side. "Sit here, and keep your eyes on his face."

"What—" I started, stopped. "What do I say?"

"I don't care! Anything, just make sure he knows he has a reason to not die on us!"

I swallowed, put my hands on his face, my forehead touching his. "Greg," I said, "if you die, I will literally follow you into whatever afterlife there is and drag you back kicking and screaming."

"Jesus Christ, Meg," Virgil muttered.

"You said give him a reason," I snapped.

"Do you take everything to extremes?" Virgil said. "Don't answer that, you're distracting me. His invincibility is making pulling his ribs out of his lungs really hard." There was a cracking groan, and Greg's chest popped back into place. "Fuck," Virgil said. "Okay, Meg, move out of the way, and don't look. I need to get the fluid out of his lungs." I turned, huddled with my back facing them.

I'm not sure I've heard anything worse before.

"We're good," Virgil finally said. "He's breathing again. I think I can wait to set the arm. Give me my keys; I don't trust you not to accidentally hit us with the car."

I handed him the keys. His hands were shaking. "But you were going to trust me to drive it away?" I asked.

"Yeah, because I figured I was going to be dead and wouldn't care," he said. "Don't move. I'm going to bring it over here so I can load him in."

It took Virgil three tries to get Greg lifted. Sweating and shaking, he finally got him into the passenger seat that we had leaned back as far as it could go.

"Are you okay?" I asked him.

"I'm having to pull an invincible man back into one piece and keep him that way, so no, I am not okay. Just because you can rip people apart without any effort doesn't mean the rest of us don't need to use it to pick up the pieces left behind."

I bristled and started to open my mouth to shoot back a retort, but Virgil sighed. I hesitated.

"I'm sorry, Meg," he said. "That was uncalled for. Get in, I need to get him back to my lab."

"Will he make it that far?"

"I'll make sure he will," he said. "We can't take him to a hospital anyway, what are they going to do? They can't get anything through his skin."

I climbed in behind the driver's seat and sat, twisted to face Greg, one hand on his face, the other with my fingers curled in his hair. Virgil got in after me and sat for a minute after the engine turned over. "Are we forgetting something?" he asked, his eyes on the snack stand. "Eh, doesn't matter," and he hit the gas.

∞

Greg wasn't in much better shape than I was from my own rescue. Having his invincibility turned back on him had done a number on him. Virgil wouldn't tell me the full extent of the damage. Fortunately for him, and Virgil, once Virgil had him pieced back together, his body seemed pretty determined to stay that way. Especially since once he had gotten Greg's arm to cooperate and shift back together the way it was supposed to be, Virgil had passed out from the effort it had taken.

It had taken me a while to get him to wake up from that, and then he had told me to just leave him on the floor because Greg was already in the only hospital bed. I wouldn't have been able to lift him anyway, so it was probably for the best.

When Greg hadn't woken up after a couple of days, Virgil locked me out of the lab. He said it was because he needed to figure out how to get IV fluids into him, but I knew that wasn't it. Because I had already done a midnight wandering – unable to sleep the first night back – and had found him spooning water down Greg's throat. He had come out gray-faced but smiling hours later and told me Greg had woken briefly, and the first thing he did was ask about me. Virgil had assured him I was fine, and Greg had fallen asleep again, but it appeared he was out of the woods.

Greg was awake when I came in the next morning bearing coffee, scrambled eggs and toast. All made courtesy of Virgil, because I can't cook. His face lit up. "Meg," he croaked. I was going to have to make Virgil come check his lungs when he came back in with the way he sounded.

"Greg," I said, setting the tray of food on his lap.

He snaked his good arm around my waist and pulled me toward him. "Watch the coffee!" I yelped. But he had already knocked the entire tray out of the way with his other hand, and I pretended not to hear him hiss as I landed on his chest. Slowly, he wrapped his broken arm around me.

"You," he murmured into my hair, "you were supposed to run."

"But did I die?" I asked. "And technically, I did run, just not in the direction you told me to."

He huffed out a laugh, then groaned. I tried to slide back off him; it didn't sound like his ribs were ready to take any sort of weight. "I'm fine," he insisted.

"That's my line," I told him.

"Stop making me laugh," he said.

We were silent while he held me, my head resting on his shoulder.

"Where's Virgil?" he asked eventually.

"Outside, burning the contents of his room."

Greg nodded and then subsided, closing his eyes.

"So," I said because it was too quiet again. "Are we both unemployed now?" I was kind of responsible for the murder of a hero, so I wasn't sure where that left me in terms of not, you know, rotting in some sort of super villain prison. Hard to hold a job if you're on the run. And promises we made aside, I don't know that any of us actually expected to live through that final encounter.

"Hmm, I think we can count ourselves freelance," Greg said.

"I don't remember ever agreeing to be a hero," I said. "In fact, I distinctly remember someone promising to get the hero recruitment to stop."

"Well, you did kind of just save the world from whatever Red Eye had in store for it if he had gotten your power."

"Yup, once is enough. Never again."

Greg chuckled, and then groaned again. "The rocket launcher hurt less," he said.

"That seems kind of unfair. Invincibility, but you can still feel the pain?"

"Hmm," he said. He kissed the top of my head. "Could be worse."

He was asleep again when Virgil finally came back in. "How's our patient?" He asked, coming around to the other side of the bed and then sighing when he almost stepped in the remnants of the dishes and food.

"Wasn't me," I told him.

"Seems wrong to make him pay for it," Virgil said, hands over the side he could reach, Greg had asked me to stay, so I was still in his arms, and there was no way I was getting up.

Look, I'm comfortable there. I can absolutely move Greg's arms off me and out of the way if I need to. I just don't want to.

"Are his lungs okay?" I asked.

"They're fine. He's going to be sore for a while though."

"What about—" and I hesitated.

"Bolt? I'm setting things up so it looks like Red Eye got her when she was supposed to be bringing you in. You'll be in the clear. Not sure I can do much about the fact that she told them Greg went AWOL instead of following orders, but since things turned out for the best, they may just, what is it? Welcome him back with open arms?"

"He mentioned something about going freelance."

"Well, once he heals up, we'll discuss it. He's going to need a new base of operations anyway, and I could use some team members."

"Members?"

"I could use someone like you, Meg."

"Not a hero," I told him.

"Not a hero," he agreed. "More like, Vengeance?"

"Who's Vengeance?" Greg asked, his eyes still closed.

"Meg is," Virgil told him.

"I am not."

"That's what the Furies were, Meg. They were Vengeance."

I scowled at him. I had told him what had happened when I had gone after Red Eye, what the whispers and figures had wanted. About both the torment and the vengeance they were calling for. He had spent the next few hours searching through his books and then dropped one about Greek myths in my lap, open to the page about the Furies. He had been like a dog with a bone ever since. It had given me pause, wondering if my parents knew what I was, what my power was, when they had named me after one of the Furies. At least they hadn't gone with Alecto.

I hadn't told Virgil about the sand, the sea and the olive grove I was seeing in my dreams. There was a memory there, just out of reach.

The silence stretched, until I finally huffed, "Fine. But I'm not saving the world."

ABOUT THE AUTHOR

Jamie lives in Charlotte, NC with her husband, three feral children and two badly behaved dogs.

She has BAs in English and Theatre, her favorite part of which was working backstage on traveling Broadway productions.

25056092R00144